A Promise of Home

Susanne Bellamy

DEDICATION

To my big sister, Gillian, with love

.

ACKNOWLEDGMENTS

As always, many thanks to my editor and critique partner, Annie Seaton, for her support and enthusiasm and guidance. You make my work shine!

.

Chapter One

The faded sign indicating Lark Creek, population one thousand, seven hundred and thirty-four—*one thousand, seven hundred and thirty-five if you include me*—loomed out of the darkness. Katy Leonard sighed, a sound filled with sorrow and regret . . . and guilt.

Why did I wait so long?

The moonless night pressed in on all sides until she turned onto Main Street and, for the first time in her twenty-five years, took a hard look at the deserted heart of the only place she'd truly called home. Papered-over windows like the closed eyelids of the dead lined both footpaths, and there were more empty shops than occupied. More than likely the occupants of the cemetery outnumbered the souls living in town. A shiver ran down her spine, and a band tightened around her lungs.

She glanced at the squat, velvet-wrapped box strapped into the front passenger seat. Tears stung her eyes, but anger burned in her heart. Bringing Gran home should have been a family affair, but they had all left her to scatter the ashes alone.

She wiped a hand over her damp cheek.

At the roundabout where Leonard Drive, named for an earlier ancestor of her family, intersected with the main road, she averted her eyes from the shiny new panel on the war memorial, and turned right.

Light shone from only one house as the car wound along the road towards the creek, but the headlights picked out long grass and a faded 'house for rent' sign before she turned into the driveway of

Rose Cottage, the last house before Leonard Drive turned left and became Creek Road.

A headache thudded behind Katy's eyes as twin beams of light lit the house and front garden. The Queenslander sat high on stumps with a broad veranda running across the front where she used to sit and share her hopes and dreams with Gran. Either side of the wide front stairs a pair of overgrown bushes crouched like Chinese guardian lions on the terrace before the ground sloped gently towards the fence and on down to Lark Creek.

Tired and sad and anxious about the responsibility that was hers alone, Katy parked in the garage. Was the power still on, or would she need the portable gas lantern she'd brought with her?

She turned to her precious package. "Well, Gran, here we are, home again."

Once inside the house, Katy felt around for the light switch. Led by instinct and memory she sighed with relief as the old-fashioned forty-watt kitchen bulb shed its puny light. Gran hadn't believed in wasting money, but Katy liked to be able to see. Tomorrow she'd see about replacing the bulbs with new, brighter LED lights. On the table lay a note and Katy raised it to read in the uncertain light.

'Pie in fridge and a litre of milk. Come over for a cup of tea when you have time. Bessie.'

Gran's neighbour had been her best friend since school and their friendship had spanned sixty years and the loss of both their husbands. Katy smiled, suddenly feeling not quite so alone.

She surveyed the kitchen with the huge black wood burner that Gran had refused to part with even after Katy's Dad had installed an electric oven, the cupboard doors in four alternating pastel colours, the scrubbed pine chairs and the table where Gran had taught her to cook and listened to her fears about her mother's new marriage. She blinked away tears and sniffed. The new fridge Gran had purchased last Christmas when the old one gave up the ghost, looked out of place in the old-fashioned room.

Hugging Gran's ashes to her chest, Katy wandered along the hallway, flicking on light switches as she went, but not even turning on every light until the house was lit up like a Christmas tree could push back the gloom of her homecoming.

Stale air hung in rooms too long closed up in the late spring heat and a line of sweat trickled down her spine. After setting Gran's ashes on the mantelpiece in the lounge room, Katy opened the leadlight-edged windows and latched them on the widest hole of their metal arms. Light spilled onto the wide front veranda, casting elongated red, green, and yellow diamonds across the faded white cane chair where Gran had sat on hot summer nights.

Katy gripped the window ledge and her vision blurred again.

Hands in pockets, she strolled onto the veranda and sank into the cane armchair. She curled her legs up and listened to the strident cicada song and the occasional annoying buzz of a mosquito. In the quiet distance, water trickled and splashed over the remnants of the tiny waterfall up Lark Creek near the Roberts' land. It was all so achingly familiar. And so heartbreakingly different. Without Gran, how could she stay here where so many happy memories had been made?

But without an income how can I afford to keep her home?

Chapter Two

Katy woke and stretched beneath the pink and purple sheets Gran had let her choose one Christmas holiday years ago. Katy smoothed the fabric and smiled at the memory of buying the sheet set, and Gran patting her shoulder when she asked if *so much colour* was okay. During school terms, she and her older sister, Rosemary, had lived with Mum and her new husband—Katy's lip curled and she shuddered at the memory—in his minimalist, wedding-cake-white mansion. White House McMansion was a nightmare. White everywhere—except when she'd tracked mud across the stupid, *who'd-have-white-anyway* carpet after her footy team had won their semi-final. 'Excitement is no excuse for sloppiness, Katherine. You will miss next week's game as punishment.' She'd missed the finals and her mother's words—barbed words that, without the softening influence of Dad's love had slowly eroded her self-confidence—stung even after all this time.

Gran, bless her, was the polar opposite.

Missing Dad when he left on another tour in Afghanistan and united in their dislike of Mum's new husband, Gran had made Rose Cottage their home.

A gentle knocking on the front door brought Katy to her feet. She grabbed her phone, surprised to see it was already eight a.m. "Coming," she called as she pulled a loose summer dress over her head and raced to answer the door.

She opened it to see her nearest neighbour smiling at her. "Bessie, good morning. Lovely to see you."

Small and sprightly, Bessie Jenkins had been like a great aunt to her and Rosie. Bessie was the same age as Gran, but she still walked three or four kilometres every day and had been a regular at the town swimming pool.

Until it closed.

"Hello, Katy. I hope it's not too early to be dropping in. How are you, dear?" She drew Katy into a hug that warmed and welcomed her, and she forgot how lonely this homecoming had been.

"Fine. Come in. Would you like a cuppa?"

"I shouldn't . . ."

"But you will." She grinned as the usual exchange between Gran and Bessie fell from her mouth. "You'll have to excuse any mess. We only got in last night after dark."

Bessie took her arm and Katy looked into her neighbour's concerned eyes. "We? Did you come down with someone? I thought you said on the phone you were coming alone. I don't want to put you out if you have a guest. Oh, no, not at all."

Katy turned and looked through the open doorway at the box containing Gran's ashes and sorrow clutched her heart as the reality of her loss crashed over her again, turning her world upside down like a dumping wave. She pressed her lips together and blinked away moisture before linking her arm through Bessie's. "Just me—and Gran's ashes."

Bessie gazed at the velvet-wrapped box tied with silk cord. "Is that—"

"Yes. It might sound silly, but I was talking to Gran on the drive in last night and it made it—less lonely for a little while."

"It's not silly. I talk to Fred every time I visit the cemetery and I feel the same. Between you and me, I don't hold with what Reverend Jones claims about an afterlife. I believe Fred's spirit is hanging around and keeping an eye out for me, and Merle won't leave you to fend for yourself either. Mark my words, Katy, I can feel her presence in the house."

"Um, great." How she felt about living with a ghost, even a friendly one, Katy didn't want to think about as she led the way into the kitchen. It was creepy, even though in some bizarre way it comforted her.

Bright morning light revealed what the dim overhead light had hidden. A thick layer of dust covered every flat surface and had even insinuated its way into the glass-panelled china cupboard. "Have a seat. I'll put the kettle on."

Bessie ran a finger through the dust on the bench top. "I should have thought to pop in and tidy up after I fed Merle's chooks yesterday. They've been producing lots of eggs lately."

"You've got more than enough to do looking after your place. Besides, cleaning will keep me busy until I work out what to do with Gran's house."

Bessie gasped. "Never tell me you're thinking of selling Merle's home?"

Katy plugged in the kettle. *Crap, crap, crap, why did I say anything?*

She dragged in a deep breath and exhaled slowly. According to *Big Sister* Rosie, Katy was many things—irresponsible and unable to settle, and saving for a rainy day was beyond her comprehension—but she wouldn't lie. "Honestly? I don't want to sell it, but how can I afford to keep it?"

Saying goodbye to Gran's home after leaving Gran scattered around her rose bush would be difficult. Maybe impossible. The thought of driving away from the only home she'd truly known made her stomach clench, but if she couldn't find a job quickly or some way to make the house turn a profit, what choice did she have? As far as she'd been able to discover, there were no carer positions, live-in or otherwise, available nearby and she was between jobs. Again.

Rosie said I've switched jobs too often since Dad died.

Water bubbled furiously in the kettle and the automatic switch turned it off. "Tea or coffee, Bessie?"

"A strong cup of tea. God knows I need it." Bessie sank into her usual seat, her hands clasped and resting on the table. She muttered something that might have been, "I don't want to die here alone." Guilt joined the loss swirling in Katy's stomach. Too aware of Bessie's steady gaze following her as she washed and dried Gran's bone china cups, Katy avoided meeting Bessie's eyes as she set a little jug of milk on the table. Sixty years ago the red and yellow rose patterned service had been Grandpa's gift to his new bride. It remained as bright and fresh today as it had back then.

When the tea had brewed, Katy slid into a chair and poured two cups. Handing one to Bessie, she asked, "Do you have any ideas how I can make Gran's house earn money?"

Bessie stirred half a teaspoon of sugar into her tea and took a sip before she set the cup on its saucer. "Maybe. I was watching television the other night. It was one of those home renovation shows that seem so popular with city people. They talked about *repurposing* buildings."

"What, like turning old warehouses into lofts and apartments? How would that help me?"

"Well, what if you got on that show and did up Merle's home?"

"I need more money than is in my bank account to buy paint let alone pay for the sorts of building work they do on those shows."

Bessie grinned as she touched Katy's hand. "But that's the beauty of this show. If they think a project has potential, *they* put up an amount of money and then it's up to the homeowner to spend it wisely."

"That's pretty cool. But how do I *repurpose* Gran's home? I mean, what need is there that it would fill? Lark Creek isn't anyone's idea of a tourist destination. What is there in this part of the world to attract people?"

"What if you found something here in Lark Creek that would make people want to come here instead of heading for the coast? After all, Travis Roberts likes Lark Creek enough to come back and settle here."

"Travis? You mean he's back for good?" She glanced through the back door. Trees and a hilly paddock hid the Roberts' farm house from her view, but she'd visited his parents enough times with Gran to see their high-set home clearly in her mind's eye.

And Travis Roberts.

Her heartbeat kicked up a notch as she recalled his perfect face and sexy smile. How could she ever forget his smile? The way it crinkled the corners of his hazel eyes and invaded her adolescent dreams when she returned to McMansionland had inspired one of her later rebellions. His poster had graced the wall above her bed for precisely one day before her mother removed it, but each night she'd taken it from its hiding place in her desk drawer, unfolded it and daydreamed. Travis' smile reminded her of Lark Creek and Gran and happier times. It was the sort of smile dreams were made of.

And now, if what Bessie said was true, Travis was back and living just over the hill from Rose Cottage. He was her neighbour, and neighbours did neighbourly things—like calling on one another.

"Why don't you drive around the district and get a bit of a feel for what's here. Maybe something will pop into your mind. Your dad's motorbike is still in the shed. Merle couldn't bear to part with it." Bessie sipped her tea, but Katy felt the weight of expectation sitting heavy in the sideways glances her neighbour cast.

"Thanks for the suggestion, Bessie. I'll look into that show, see what the conditions of entry are, and see if I can come up with an idea that grabs their attention. Biscuit? Only store-bought, I'm sorry."

"You do that, Katy, and maybe you could talk to your handsome neighbour. No one's seen him since he came back to town." Bessie took her time selecting a biscuit as though it were the most important decision of the moment. Katy wasn't fooled by her pseudo-casualness. Bessie was up to something, but what it might be eluded her. Katy shrugged and chose a biscuit too.

"Is that so?" She had Dad's motorbike. Maybe she'd take it on a trip along the creek and up the back paddock and give it a test run? And if she happened to run into Travis Roberts while she was riding? A flicker of excitement—and, dare she imagine, hope—raced through her body.

If Travis was back in Lark Creek and willing to be featured on her segment of the television show, he might just be the perfect attraction.

Chapter Three

Travis bent over the bay horse's hoof and plied the hoof pick. Mercury whuffled and nudged his shoulder. "Good boy, nearly done. I've got some apple for you when I've finished. You like apples, don't you, boy?" Mercury nickered in pleasure when Travis let go of the horse's hoof and patted his side. A kind of peace settled around them as he tidied away his tools and offered a piece of apple. He wiped his hands on a small towel and grimaced at the sting of his latest cut.

Imagining his manager, Kyle, freaking out and making comments like *take care of your hands* gave him grim pleasure. Because, of course, none of it mattered. Not anymore. Since the accident, his fine motor skills had disappeared up shit creek. If there'd been a paddle, he wouldn't have been able to ply it properly.

And even if his damaged hand could play his guitar, who would pay good money to come and see him with a face like his? He frowned and a familiar ball of tension lodged in his gut at the thought of facing anyone ever again.

I'm turning into old man Muggeridge up the valley. Nobody sees him from one year's end to the other either.

Mercury whickered and nodded his head as though he totally understood Travis.

Maybe he did.

Animals were intuitive, and didn't judge a man on his appearance. Which explained why he found himself spending big chunks of time each day with his horse. He took Mercury's halter off and hung it on the hook. "We'll go for another ride tomorrow, but right now there's a fence I need to—"

The roar of a motorbike engine caught his attention. The engine misfired, grating on his sense of timing before the approach of a vehicle from the direction of the back paddock registered.

Back paddock? Who could have gained access to his property through the back gate? One of the first jobs he'd attended to had been ensuring the fences were secure with a remote-controlled, lockable front gate. Nothing like good fences to keep stock in—and people out.

But some local lout had discovered the unsecured back gate and was trespassing. With a grunt of annoyance, Travis tossed the towel he'd wiped his hands on into the washing container and strode out of the barn. The motorbike stopped on the far side of the house near the front door and Travis' gut churned. A trespasser wouldn't stop and call in at the house. A trespasser would charge on through his property making as much noise as possible and leaving a trail of sliding tyre marks as he slewed around bends.

"Hello?" The voice was female. His heart slammed against his ribcage. *Not a trespasser. A god damn visitor.*

And a female visitor at that.

Who?

I'm not ready for this.

His agent's voice echoed in his head—*you'll never be ready to meet people as long as you hide out there in the boondocks.*

As quietly as possible he changed direction and climbed the back steps, locking the door behind him before creeping—*in his own house, damn it!*—along the hallway and into the small office to the right of the front door. He flattened himself against the wall and peered through a narrow gap in the curtains. A woman stood at his door with her back to him, swinging a helmet by the chin strap and looking over the paddocks. Hair the deep dark black-red of Christmas cherries was pulled into a low ponytail.

She turned towards the door, raised her hand and knocked again.

"Anyone home?"

Lordy, but she was beautiful. A long-forgotten memory whispered through his mind. . . Music, crowds—he was sure he'd been singing as he tried to place who she was. Somewhere, sometime, he'd met her . . . but she looked different, more grown up now. Was that it?

His last Christmas holiday in Lark Creek roared back in vivid colour as he remembered. Little Katy Leonard. The last time he'd seen her she'd been fourteen or fifteen years old, on the cusp of becoming a woman. What he best remembered was the way her grandmother had slid a protective arm around her shoulders when he'd come off stage after performing at a local charity show. Back then Katy had been pretty with the promise of what she might become. Grownup Katy was a stunner.

His grimaced. At least, the uninjured side of his face still tightened. The scarred side of his face was puckered and mostly immobile. It was enough to send children screaming and little old ladies fainting if they saw it. Saw him.

There was no way he'd open the door to Katy Leonard, today or ever. Whatever she wanted, she could whistle until the cows came home. He was having nothing to do with her or anyone.

***

Disappointed no one answered her knock Katy stepped back from the door. Something flickered in the window to her left and she turned to look. A pair of closed curtains filled the square panes of old fashioned sash windows. She strolled to the window and glanced around the edges, wondering if a moth was trapped between the material and the glass. She saw nothing but a sliver of desk through a chink in the curtains, but she couldn't rid herself of the notion someone was watching her.

All Bessie's talk of ghosts has me jumping at shadows.

Telling herself she was made of sterner stuff, she walked down the stairs, refusing to look at the window . . . just in case old Mr Roberts' ghost peered back at her. She clipped on her helmet and flicked up the kickstand. But as she eased off the clutch she couldn't help a quick glance at the window. Her breath caught in her throat. A single eye watched her through the gap in the curtains. She jerked the clutch and snuffed the engine. Her head rocked back at the abrupt stop. She turned quickly and stared at the window. There was no one there. Was it a trick of the light? An odd reflection?

Her heart hammered in her chest, beating a tattoo against her ribs. This was ridiculous. Grief and worry were firing up her imagination. No one was hiding behind the curtains. No one was watching her. She needed to leave and come back when she was rested and less inspired by Bessie's ghost stories.

She breathed deeply—exhaled. Concentrating on driving safely rather than trying to catch a mysterious hidden watcher would serve her better. She released the clutch and set off along the narrow path, down the back paddock and through the gate onto the road that curved past Rose Cottage and ran beside the creek most of the way to the vineyard.

By the time she drew up in front of the winery owned by Geilis Romney's family, she had mastered her paranoia. Pulling off her helmet, she shook her head and fluffed her flattened hair.

"Hat hair—it's the pits, isn't it?" A figure stepped into view at her side. A familiar and very welcome figure.

"Geilis! I'm so happy to see you." Katy dropped her helmet and swung her leg over the tank of the motorbike in time to fall into her friend's arms.

"Hey, sweetie, I'm so, so sorry I couldn't be at your gran's funeral. How are you doing?"

Tears sprang into Katy's eyes, but she blinked them away. She'd cried enough tears to turn Lark Creek into a flooding river. "Okay, I guess. Or not. Rosie's left me with the task of spreading Gran's ashes." She stepped out of Geilis' hug and turned to remove the keys from the ignition.

"By yourself? Heartless bitch."

Katy shrugged. "She's tied up with work at the laboratory. They're chasing some big grant money, she and Geoff are off to Japan in a few days and she said she can't get away." Katy hardly believed the excuse any more, but Geilis' raised eyebrow expressed what Katy would never say aloud. Excusing her older sister's absence to Gran had become habit when Rosie stopped coming for long visits once she went to university, but it didn't stop the hurt and a deep-seated anger that surprised Katy. Was she angry with her sister for leaving her to spread Gran's ashes all alone, or was she angry with Gran for leaving her?

"That's a poor excuse not to make the drive out. What would it cost her? A day on a weekend to honour your gran." Geilis' sharp tone dismissed Rosie, but then she'd never clicked with Katy's sister. Where people were concerned, Geilis rarely changed her mind and Rosie had got up her nose the first time they met.

Maybe the ten-year age difference was to blame for their lack of connection. It hadn't been an issue for Katy until recently. Until Gran's will was read leaving Rose Cottage solely to Katy.

Was that the reason? Was Rosie jealous, or angry that she got Gran's shares and I got the house?

She'd tried, but making sense of Gran's decision was beyond her while she had to face up to scattering the ashes by herself. "I'm not sure when I'll do it, or if I'll even be able to when the time comes. And if I do, should I have some sort of ceremony?"

Pity filled Geilis' bright green eyes. "Do what feels right to you. And Katy, you know I'll be there by your side when you—"

Katy slung an arm over Geilis' shoulder at the hitch in her friend's voice. "What's wrong?"

"Nothing. Hay fever." Geilis pulled a tissue from her pocket and blew her nose, but her eyes were suspiciously pink. "Come on inside and have a glass of last season's vintage. It's my first solo effort and my last assignment for my oenology degree. I got a Distinction for it."

In a way, knowing that Geilis missed Gran almost as much as Katy did helped. Katy linked her arm through her friend's and together they entered the tasting room. High ceilings with exposed wooden beams and second-hand bricks created a sense of timelessness, but the public area was a new addition since the girls had finished high school. Katy sat at a small round table beside the folding doors, closed until visitors arrived while Geilis explored the contents of the fridge behind the counter.

She drew the vacuum seal from the neck before carrying the half-empty bottle of white wine to the table. "This one is mine, my first wine baby." Geilis crooned as she poured two glasses, set the bottle on the table between them and raised her glass. "To Merle Leonard, a lovely lady and wonderful friend."

"To Gran." Katy touched her glass to Geilis' and sipped the wine. It could have been vinegar for all she could taste with her stuffy nose and choky throat, but she smiled as she set her glass down. "Well done and congrats, wine girl. I envy you."

"Me? Why?"

"You know what you want to do, who you want to be. I feel like I'm—I don't know—stumbling around in the dark hoping I'll walk into my life." Adrift on a sea of loss and despair since Dad had been killed, no job, no place had seemed enough reason to put down roots. There was no point in staying too long—getting close to anyone. But Gran's gift would—might change that.

Putting down roots— She shivered. Or was that really what she was looking for? The idea frightened the heck out of her.

Geilis gestured with the hand holding her glass, taking in everything around them and met Katy's gaze. "I hate to tell you but you're in it now."

"God, Geilis, it's a nightmare. When Dad was killed last year, Gran and I still had each other but now she's gone and I feel so lost. Walking into Gran's home and not seeing her, not having her hugging me, not hearing her voice—it felt so wrong. It felt like a piece of me was missing."

And I have to spread her ashes and work out what to do with her cottage.

Geilis wrapped Katy's hand around her glass and lifted it a little. "Drink, taste the wine and think of something positive. Seen any good-looking men lately?"

"Damn it, I won't keep feeling sorry for myself." Katy blinked away morose tears. She'd had enough of crying and feeling hollow. Geilis' question reminded her of her abortive visit to her neighbour on the hill. She sniffed, drank some wine and looked at Geilis. "Tell me, what have you heard about Travis Roberts coming home?"

Geilis shot her a look of surprise. "I didn't know he had. Who told you he'd come back?"

"Bessie. She said he's happily settled back in Lark Creek and who wouldn't want to live here."

"Weird. I wonder why she'd say that, about him wanting to live here?"

"Probably because I was moaning about not knowing what to do with Gran's home. I promise—no more moaning . . . maybe one more lot when I spread Gran's ashes in her garden."

Geilis set her glass on the table and covered Katy's free hand. Her fingers were cool, but firm, and her green gaze was insistent. "Sweetie, it's not your Gran's home now. It's yours."

It's yours, it's yours, yours . . . Not Gran's, because Gran wasn't there. Not in any form Katy could wrap her arms around.

"She really is gone, isn't she? What am I going to do about— my home, Geilis?" The words stumbled off her tongue, tripping as they took their first tentative steps into the world.

My home, it's my home now.

Geilis squeezed her hand and pushed Katy's glass closer. "You don't have to rush into a decision immediately. There isn't money owing on the property, is there?"

Katy shook her head, picked up her glass and sipped. "No, but you know what I've been doing. I only worked full-time for a couple of years after I finished my social work degree, but since Dad died—I threw in my job and I've been filling in when a live-in carer goes on holiday. The pay hasn't been great, and soon there'll be rates and insurance and—and bills. And I don't have a job at the moment."

"Calm down. It'll be fine. You're upset about your gran dying, and the ashes and your horrid sister leaving you to do the hard stuff, but the house isn't going anywhere. You've time to think what

15

you want to do with her gift."

Katy pulled a tissue from her pocket and blew her nose. "You're right."

Time. That was one thing she had plenty of. And energy and two hands with which to shape her future.

"I had half an idea last night. Don't laugh, but—what if I turned Rose Cottage into a B and B?"

Chapter Four

"Hey, Katy, this is the big opportunity I told you about. The grant has come through for the Japan trip. Adam isn't happy about coming with Geoff and me, but it's a brilliant chance for him to immerse himself in another culture. I told you he started learning Japanese this year, didn't I?" Rosie sounded upbeat and more jovial than usual, as though she was trying to sound the same as before.

Late afternoon sun slanted under the eaves as Katy wandered onto the veranda, phone pressed to her ear as her older sister's voice continued.

"Yes, you did." Resentment flickered briefly in Katy's breast. Everything came easily to Rosie; she had a husband who adored her, a fulfilling job, and a comfortable life. She knew who she was and where she was going; she was a good mother to Adam. After their own mother's disinterest had sent them into the country to Gran, they'd promised to always be there for each other, come hell or high water, and never to palm their children off on family because they were a *nuisance*. Funny how that word always announced itself in her mother's bored tone of voice. But Rosie's life wasn't what Katy wanted for herself. Could she restore her enjoyment and love of social work here in Lark Creek?

Clinging to the positives, Katy tried to match Rosie's upbeat tone. "Lucky Adam. What a terrific opportunity for him. Why doesn't he want to go?"

"He says it's the idea of living in a one-bedroom apartment with his parents and having to finish the school year with home schooling lessons while we're there, but I think it's more about him not wanting to be away from his school mates for so long. He's at that age where parents don't know anything and friends are the fount of all wisdom." A wistful note crept into Rosie's voice, surprising and barely there, but noticeable because Rosie never allowed negative thinking to colour her life.

"How long will you be in Japan? He could come out here for a visit if he wanted to? There's the creek for swimming although there isn't much water in it. Does he still enjoy painting?" Katy smiled at the memory of her nephew's efforts to paint the walls of his bedroom when he was twelve. Surely his skills had improved since then. "There's heaps of painting to do in the house, the garden is running riot and—"

"What are you suggesting? Do you think I'm angling for the same deal as our mother conned Gran into?" Was that a hitch in Rosie's breathing? Was she annoyed? Angry? Her big sister valued work and family. She'd looked after Katy when their parents divorced and got on with whatever life threw at her. But that hitch in her breath worried Katy.

"Rosie? What's wrong? I didn't mean it to sound like that."

"Nothing. Not a thing." But the ragged breath that came through the phone said otherwise. "Look, it's nice of you to offer, but we always said we'd never do what our mother did. I'm really looking forward to seeing Nagoya with Adam. We'll be back in Oz in late January at the latest, in time for the start of the school year. Maybe we'll drive out for a visit before Adam goes back to school."

"Sure." Maybe was a cop-out word, a means to procrastinate or delay what didn't fit into one's life.

Maybe I'll drive out to Lark Creek when I get back from camping, Gran.

Casually delaying her planned visit to Gran had seemed nothing at the time because time stretched endlessly and forever ahead of her. But Gran had passed away the night before she got back from camping with friends; she knew it would haunt her till the end of her days. Never again would Katy put self before family because tomorrow wasn't guaranteed. Gazing out towards the creek she repeated her response. "Sure. That will be lovely if you can make it." Except for Gran's unconditional love—*and Dad's love*—her family relationships were fraught. She ended the call and leaned on the railing.

Down by the creek a pair of magpie-larks swooped and soared, their duet calls—the call of home—tumbling into one another as they caught dinner. Gold light gilded the trees along the bank and the familiarity of the scene so often shared with Gran soothed her unquiet spirit. She could truly make this her home if she tried.

Carefree Katy, careless Kate—the childhood nicknames floated in her mind. Had it been Rosie who gave them to her? Probably. And she'd earned them. Dad's death had triggered something in her so that throwing in a good job and wandering wherever a casual position came up had seemed perfectly reasonable. Security was an illusion and getting close to people only led to hurt when they left her.

No more. Gran's gift changed all that.

She would find a way to renovate the house. Would the B & B idea be enough to qualify her as a contender for the television show? She made a mug of coffee and carried it and her laptop back onto the veranda. Redolent with scents from the garden it was a pleasant place to make her plans for the transformation of Rose Cottage. First task was to make a list. Rosie made endless lists and she seemed to manage a highly responsible job and a family with apparent ease.

By the time Katy had drunk her coffee, her list had a grand total of three items and her mind had wandered to the creek. Was it deep enough to swim in? Was the old rope swing usable? Would guests at her B & B care? Wrenching her attention back to the screen, she sighed. How hard could it be to make a decent list? Tapping her fingernail against her tooth she looked at item number one. 'Buy groceries'.

She picked up her phone and opened the shopping list app. There. That was an easy, sensible place to start. Once that list was complete, she added three columns to a fresh page headed, 'B & B proposal' and entered *Katy enjoys cooking* in the positive column. That was a promising tick on the B & B idea. At least she could feed her guests well.

But another part of her mind niggled and nagged and demanded answers. Yes, she could cook well, but how would she entice guests? What would attract them to Lark Creek in the first place? When she and Rosie had visited Gran they'd never done the tourist thing, but maybe a drive around the district as Bessie had suggested would throw up an idea or two. She could start looking now on the drive to Dalton for groceries. And then she and her laptop were going to settle in for a thorough bout of research.

Chapter Five

Travis gripped the hoe and attacked the hard-packed soil of what had once been his mother's herb garden, now run to seed and weed. He assumed Katy Leonard was visiting her grandmother, but why had she turned up here? She'd only been a kid of fifteen or so when he'd lived here. Their circle of friends had been different and besides, she and her older sister were holiday blow-ins. But he remembered Katy and those blue eyes of hers when she'd asked for his autograph after his *farewell to Lark Creek-hello big city* concert. Her eyes were the blue of summer skies surrounded by a deeper blue, like the sea before a storm.

If he'd opened the door he'd have known why she'd come calling. But he'd worked hard not to see anyone since he'd returned to Lark Creek. Not even the delivery guy who brought his groceries to the house every week had seen him. And if he'd opened the door, by now half the population of Lark Creek would have been on his doorstep, curious to see his injuries. He refused to be the freak show.

He attacked a thick clump of thorny weeds, relishing the flex of muscle each time he raised the hoe. Last week he'd managed only fifteen minutes of hoeing before his hands turned to jelly. Today he'd done—he stopped, his breathing only a little ragged as he pulled out his phone and checked the time—twenty minutes and he had energy for more. Maybe his hand was continuing to improve.

As he flexed and fisted his right hand, a brief burst of optimism flared and when the phone vibrated in his left hand and his manager's name appeared on the screen, he pressed the button to accept the call without thinking. "Hi, Kyle, what's up?"

"Trav, is that really you or have you recorded a personalised message just to shut me up?"

In spite of Travis' stubborn refusal to answer, Kyle had phoned every few days, not haranguing, not persuading. Just letting Travis know he was on the other end of the line—whenever he decided to pick up his phone. "It's me in the flesh, mate."

"How are you doing?" Kyle's hearty tone had grated through the days in hospital while Travis recovered from surgery on his hand, but today, it was good to hear his voice. Maybe Kyle was right. Maybe Travis had shut himself away for too long if a simple phone call buoyed his spirit.

"I'm okay."

"Just okay, or stronger? How're your hands?"

What could he say? Kyle asked the same questions every time he left a voice message—*how are your hands, when will you come back to Sydney, can I book your next gig?* How long would it be before his manager accepted what Travis knew already? Despite the small gains in strength he'd noticed recently, his days of performing in front of audiences were over.

"You know the accident damaged a nerve in my right hand. I'll never be able to play the same again."

"But you are able to play so adapt how you play. If musicians like Django Reinhardt did it, well—your musicianship is close to their league." Kyle's upbeat tone grated, and the analogy was crazy.

"I'm nowhere near players of his calibre and you know it." Travis wiped his forehead on his shirt sleeve and moved into the shade.

"That's a matter of opinion. Anyway, we can bring another guitarist into the backing band to fill in any bits you don't feel you can play so well, but, mate, we need to get you back in the spotlight and sooner rather than later."

"And I keep telling you that—"

"Look, I hear you, but there's this great opportunity to play in front of Simon Reeve. It could be the boost we've been looking for, the making of your international career."

"You need to accept that my performing career is over, finished, *kaput*. I can't play my own music, and my face would scare even die-hard fans. It's not going to happen." Regretting answering Kyle's call, Travis strode to the top of the garden slope and looked over the valley, seeking its calming influence.

"I'd accept your career was finished if you'd died in that accident, but you didn't. You're alive, your voice is fine and your mind is active, if still in a dark place right now. So, mate, I'm not giving up trying to convince you to perform again." There was a pause, the looming kind that filled the silence like an axe waiting to fall. Travis held his breath. "I'll be up your way in a few days. I expect coffee and cake when I get there, okay?"

"Dream on."

"Okay, coffee with a slug of something decent will do. I'll call again, but I'll see you then."

Travis shoved his phone back in his pocket and stared off into the distance. Maybe he'd not answer the door to Kyle when he arrived. It had worked with Katy Leonard.

Nah, Kyle would just thump on the door until either he broke it down or I let him in.

Travis gripped the hoe and got stuck back into weeding the herb bed. At least the plants didn't answer him back.

Chapter Six

Dithering achieved precisely nothing, unless Katy counted her growing frustration an achievement. She'd made several lists, acted on none of them, and read the rules for applying to the television show until she was sick of the legal language. After the umpteenth 'party of the first part shall blah blah blah', she gave up and simply clicked into the application form and ticked the box saying she'd read and understood the conditions.

Who reads those things all the way through anyway?

But after she filled in her details and made comments about what she wanted to achieve in Rose Cottage, she couldn't bring herself to click the send button. It was so final. What if she missed important stuff because she hadn't finished reading the many clauses in the disclaimer? Eventually, sick of second-guessing herself, she saved the document and closed the tab.

Restless and with energy to burn, she pulled on her boots and set off up the back paddock to Travis Roberts' house. His name and presence in town could tip the balance in her favour on the application. But she should talk to the man first.

Yet again, there was no answer to her knocking on his door. But there'd been fresh hoof prints in the mud puddle outside the barn. A small fall of overnight rain had muddied the ground and the track ahead showed signs of recent use. It gave Katy hope that Travis—since she was on his land—had ridden this way not long before her. She toed the edge of the nearest hoof print. It caved easily and her boot picked up another dollop of chocolate-brown mud.

Morning light slanted through the trees and outlined the leaves in gold. The air smelled fresh and the scent of the bush rose around her as Katy strode steadily up the narrow track, slightly out of breath as she climbed towards the top.

Tipping her face to the early morning sun, she stopped in the middle of the track and closed her eyes. The sun warmed her skin without overheating her and the breeze intensified the scents of the bush; eucalyptus, and a sweetly astringent smell came from a small stand of lantana. Concentrating on drawing the sweet air into her lungs her mind roamed where it would. Just for a few minutes it didn't matter if she simply thought about *being* and lived in the moment.

With a good lungful of fresh air, she opened her eyes and looked at the view through the trees. It hadn't changed much since she and Rosie had walked over the Roberts' land with Travis' father in search of flora specimens for her school project. Trees had grown taller and Mr Roberts senior had passed away in the ten years since she had last seen Travis face-to-face. But ten years hadn't dulled her memory of his face—the perfect cheekbones, his laughing light-brown eyes and a smile that said the world was his friend. She smiled wryly at the memory of his farewell performance in the CWA hall where her teenage self had fallen in love with the young singer destined for fame and national celebrity. Remembering him as he was then made it easier to contemplate talking to him today. Surely that laughing young man still existed?

She snapped off a tall grass stalk and kept walking. The stalk had a long feathery head with a slight pink tinge, and as she ran it through her fingers, it was soft on her skin.

Breathe, she reminded herself, unwilling to lose the brief moment of serenity. *Everything will turn out right.*

The sound of hoof beats and the jingle of a harness broke into her communion with nature as a horse and rider came closer and suddenly, there he was. Travis Roberts astride a big bay horse came out of the sun like a centaur.

Shading her eyes she tensed her leg muscles and waited in the middle of the track, determined to make the most of the opportunity in spite of the huge animal bearing down on her. "Hi, neighbour."

He reined in his mount and glared down at her. At least she guessed by the imperious tilt of his head that he was glaring, but she was seriously sunblind at the moment.

"What are you doing here? This is my property and you're trespassing." Anger vibrated in his voice beyond anything Katy expected.

Nerves jumped in her stomach, her mouth dried and her vaguely thought out speech fled.

"Well? Cat got your tongue?" He turned his head to the left and she flicked a glance the same way.

A flash of hindsight suggested that, just maybe, strolling around his land without asking permission wasn't the best way to open negotiations. She tried to recall something, anything she'd half-planned to tell him. "Would you believe this is a social visit? It's what neighbours do."

"Not me. I don't *do* social stuff."

"Please, Travis, if you'll just listen—."

"Not interested. Go back the way you came and don't come on my land again."

"But—."

"I don't want to see you up here again."

The bay horse took a step to the side and a couple of steps forwards. Harness jingled and suddenly the horse towered over her, filling her vision and huffing hot horsey breath in her face. With a gasp, she took a step off the track between two bushes. Her boot rolled on a stick and she fell backwards down the slope, head over tail over head, the world spinning in a kaleidoscope of bush and sky, and landed with a thump that jarred her spine and clashed her teeth together. "Ow."

Damn the man, damn and blast and . . .

"Are you okay?" A hand settled on her shoulder and heat surrounded her as Travis wrapped an arm around her back.

Pain shot down one side of her body as he helped her sit up and she gasped.

"Clearly not. Just sit still. Where does it hurt?" His tone morphed from angry to concerned. It was less glacial than before, but she didn't care. Now she was the angry one. Angry and sore and annoyed.

"Right now? All over. Did you mean that brute to push me out of the way or can't you control your horse?"

"Of course I can control my . . . Look, I'm sorry you tripped, but that wasn't my fault, or my horse's. You stepped on something and landed in the bushes and—"

Darting glances to the side she tried to twist around to check behind her. Fear curled in her stomach and sent frantic signals to her brain. She was on the ground in the middle of the Australian bush with God knew what creatures creeping towards her. "Snakes? Are there snakes out here?"

"Possibly." He slipped an arm under her knees and, with a grunt, scooped her off the ground.

"What are you doing?" Nestled against Travis' chest high above any snakes with predatory intentions, she felt . . . oddly safe . . . and breathless. His profile was more beautiful than she remembered. Ten years had added character to his face, what she could see of it.

"Taking you back to the house. I want to check if you've hurt anything and call the ambulance if necessary." He lifted her gently into the saddle and handed her the reins. As he looked up she saw his face.

His whole face.

She couldn't hold in her gasp. A jagged scar ran from the corner of his left eye and down his cheekbone. Red and angry-looking, it disappeared into his beard. There had been a brief news story . . . some kind of accident, and that he'd been taken to hospital with non-life-threatening injuries. A muscle jumped in his smooth cheek and his eyes narrowed before he turned his back, took hold of the halter and led the horse down the track. Too shocked to do more than hang on for dear life, Katy gripped the reins and the front of the saddle and stared at the back of Travis' head.

Was that why he'd been like the Phantom when she'd tried to speak with him? Her nostrils picked up the scent of horse at the same moment the horse's ears twitched, flicking away a fly and Katy's heart thumped harder.

Heaven help her she was on a horse. Travis' horse. With Travis leading her back to his house. This wasn't the way she'd planned to achieve her objective. Horses played no role in her plan, but she'd accept being unceremoniously hoisted into the saddle and not beg him to let her off just as long as he didn't let go of the halter. She gripped the saddle with trembling hands. So long as he talked to her when they reached his house. She fixed her mind on the *opportunity*. Thinking positively was the only way to get through the ride from hell.

The horse trod lightly, almost delicately behind the man, each step adding to the surreal nature of the morning. Her brain must have seized up because right now, she couldn't think of a single thing to say. Certainly her head ached, and her back was ablaze with pain, but she could feel her feet dangling either side of the horse. With a conscious effort, she felt for the stirrups and set each foot into them.

"Okay back there?" Travis turned his head and looked back at her. The right side of his face was perfect above the short black beard and his dark gaze ran over her with clinical thoroughness.

"Uh huh." Her eyes narrowed and she could feel a frown growing. Her head really did ache and it was too hard to formulate proper sentences while he coolly assessed her. She'd jarred her spine, but sensation was returning to her backside by the time they crossed the house yard and stopped beside the back stairs.

Travis took the reins from her unresisting hands and tied the horse to the railing, and then turned and lifted her out of the saddle. "Can you stand on your own or shall I carry you upstairs?" His hands held her shoulders and his eyes expressed concern, but there was an undercurrent of something she was too fuzzy to catch and name. Was it to do with how he turned his face a little, presenting her with his uninjured cheek? She blinked at him. Without another word, he carried her upstairs and set her down in a sleek, black leather recliner. He dropped to one knee in front of her.

"Katy, follow my finger." He raised his index finger like a

doctor in a television medical series, moving it from left to right, up and down while he watched her face with more attention than her last boyfriend had ever given her. Her chest felt tight as she tried to breathe normally, but being the object of his focus was unnerving.

And just a little exciting now she was no longer on his horse. The boy she'd madly crushed on as a young teen was on his knees in front of her and staring into her eyes. She ran her tongue along her top lip. "I'm fine. I'm pretty sure I'm not concussed."

"I'm not sure. You were almost catatonic when I brought you down the hill."

"I was on a horse, that's why. I've never ridden one. They scare me silly."

"Ah, that explains how you came to do such a stupid thing as fall off the track."

Had she heard him right? Had he just called her—stupid?

All thought of fluttery teenage hormones jumping in excitement vanished, replaced by an immediate if not-quite-adult desire to hit back.

"Excuse me if I don't like horses. You're the one who didn't stop your horse from pushing me over."

"Don't be ridiculous."

"Don't be such an arsehole."

He sat back on his heels and nodded. "That's better. Now you've got some colour in your cheeks again."

She opened her mouth to respond. Nothing came out until one side of his mouth, on the perfect side, lifted. Tipping her head, she finally managed to ask, "What? Were you—did you just argue with me to distract me?"

The hint of a smile clung to one side of his mouth for a couple of seconds before he pushed to his feet and left her alone. When he returned he carried a glass of water and ice and handed it to her without a word.

She sipped, and then swallowed a mouthful. Iced water sent a pain through her head and she frowned. "Brain freeze."

"Sorry. Maybe tap water would have been better. Are you feeling better now, Katy?"

"Much, thanks." In the dim recess of her mind she noticed he had used her name. How or why that came about she had no idea. She'd never thought he'd have noticed an adoring teenage fan. "But now we're chatting like this, can I ask you something?"

His eyes narrowed and any hint of interest or neighbourliness vanished. "If it's about your trespassing on my land—"

"It isn't. It's about something else entirely."

He folded his arms across his chest and looked down at her. That dark gaze bored into her and a muscle in his cheek—the smooth and beautiful cheek he presented to her—worked overtime. Words flew out of her mind as an impression grew. Travis was hiding from the world after the accident that had scarred his cheek.

Wanting to reach out and let him know she understood, she leaned forwards in the chair. Pressure on her tailbone shot pain down her legs and up her spine. Her stomach took a dive and a wave of nausea rolled over her. Eyes scrunched shut, she sucked in an audible breath.

"Katy? What's wrong?"

She swallowed, determined not to vomit in front of Travis as she reached for his hand. "Nothing. Just—help me stand."

***

Travis took her hand and slipped an arm around her waist. Beneath his fingers, her muscles tensed, and she held herself as stiff as a plank of wood. Her cold hand gripped his tightly. Clearly what he'd thought had been little more than a tumble had done some damage. "I'll take you to the doctor."

Exerting gentle pressure he tried to draw her towards the door. She took one step, and then another and stopped, her teeth digging into her lower lip. "Just give me a minute." She drew in a deep breath, released it, and straightened up.

"Okay?"

"If you wouldn't mind dropping me at home, I'd like to lie down. Nothing's broken, I'm certain of that, but my tailbone feels bruised."

"That may be, but I won't feel easy in my mind until you've seen the doctor. At the very least he can give you something for the pain."

"She."

"Pardon?"

"The doctor is a woman. Doctor Manning. Gran saw her a couple of times. And perhaps you're right. I've got nothing in the way of tablets, although maybe the pharmacy could—"

"Katy, set my mind at rest and see the doctor." He wasn't used to begging and he wasn't used to having anyone dispute his decisions. Not since before he'd made his first million anyway. But Katy was stubborn and a bit scatty—and very attractive. Her frown and the pain he read in her blue eyes meant her refusal wasn't making a whole lot of sense.

"Please?" The word slipped out of his subconscious and sat there like Bonzer entreating him to go for a walk. Bonzer, the abandoned puppy he'd loved and played with and grown up beside. And who he'd had to leave behind when he moved into the Sydney apartment.

Katy's gaze settled on his and she tipped her head a little, like she was considering her options. "Okay. But only if you promise to talk to me afterwards."

"We can talk later." Having wrung agreement from her, Travis handed her a cushion, and then lifted her in his arms and carried her to his ute. She gave a soft gasp when he picked her up before she clasped both arms around his neck.

Her fall wasn't his fault, but a little bite of guilt pricked his conscience. He *had* stopped Mercury closer than he should have. And maybe he'd communicated some of his tension to the stallion because the horse had jibed a little, but Travis had been angry. As careful as he'd been, Katy had caught him outside and she had seen his face. And when she got past her horror she'd talk and soon everyone in Lark Creek would know. The last thing he wanted was pity, from her or from people in town.

Nausea swirled in his stomach and rose in his throat. Katy's injury was forcing him into town. Into the limelight of people's curious stares and whispered horror.

He had no choice but to face people he'd known all his life, people who would *tsk-tsk* over his scar and offer sympathy and hollow encouragement.

He settled her on the cushion on the front seat and handed her the seatbelt, shut the door and walked in a daze of disbelief to the driver's side. Backing the four-wheel drive out of the shed, he wondered about her request to talk later. He didn't want *later*, and he didn't want to hang around with Katy like they were buddies.

"Why don't you tell me what you want to talk about on the way into town?"

"Are you trying to take my mind off my posterior?"

He hadn't thought about it, hadn't thought about her except as a nuisance, as the reason for the public humiliation he knew was coming when he showed his face. Even worse, she was seated on his left and looking at his scar.

Except she wasn't. Her gaze connected directly with his. There was no flicker of blue eyes down to his cheek, only a look that conveyed—gratitude?

It made him feel worse that he'd been so wrapped up in his woes he'd forgotten hers. To make up for his callous disregard, he did his best imitation of a smile. "Is it working?"

"Maybe. Actually I'm not sure the drive into town is long enough to discuss my ideas." The car bounced through a dip in the road faster than was wise. She gripped the edge of the seat and bit her bottom lip. He turned his gaze back to the road and eased back on the accelerator, but the image of Katy's mouth was seared into his brain.

Such a full lower lip, plump and pink and desirable. Her lips were made for kissing and pleasure.

Why am I thinking of kisses with Katy Leonard? She wouldn't want to kiss a man who looks as gruesome as me.

But the more he tried to stop thinking about her mouth the more he thought about it—her. A simple phrase began playing on a loop in his brain—*lips made to kiss on the girl that I miss.* A simple guitar riff drifted into his mind, and he tried the phrase against the music. He'd tweak it later, but he liked the riff. And he liked the idea of kissing Katy Leonard. He liked it a lot.

"Travis? Which doctor are you taking me to?"

Her voice interrupted his imagining and he glanced at her, his gaze instinctively dropping to her lips. "Doctor Manning. We talked about seeing her."

"Then maybe now would be a good time to turn around. You missed the turnoff to town."

"Damn. Sorry."

Focusing on making the three-point turn as smoothly as possible, he wrenched his thoughts from how Katy Leonard's lips would taste and turned down the narrow single lane bitumen strip that led from his farm into town. The main street of Lark Creek stretched ahead of them as he turned the corner and parked in front of the doctor's surgery. It seemed like half the population of town was out and about and casting interested glances their way.

The enormity of what he was about to do hit him like a sledgehammer. His gut clenched and his lungs felt as though there wasn't enough air left to fill them as his hand tightened around the door handle. Having avoided showing his face in town until now, he was about to see half the town in one hit.

And the town was about to get its first look at Travis Roberts since his accident . . . And see his ugly, scarred face.

He pushed his door open, stepped out of the car and slammed the door with unnecessary force, cringing as the loud bang seemed to echo off the buildings. *Was he trying to make everyone look at him?* With his chin lowered and eyes avoiding making eye contact, he walked around the car and helped Katy rise from the passenger seat. Keeping one hand under her elbow and the other around her waist—on his left so she partially blocked him from view—they entered the surgery.

At the counter, he waited until the middle-aged receptionist ended her phone conversation and looked up. "Ms Leonard needs to see the doctor. She's had a fall."

The receptionist's eyes widened and she smiled. "Travis Roberts, as I live and breathe. Welcome home, hon!"

"Hello, Dora." He waited for her to register his scarred cheek, waited for the predictable revulsion, waited for unwanted pity to take over and colour their encounter. He waited . . .

"Sorry to hear about your accident, but we were thrilled when we heard you'd moved back into your parents' old place." Her smile grew wider before she turned to Katy. "Hello, love. How are you doing?"

"Hi, Dora, Travis is worried I've done some damage, but—"

"Come on through. Lisa is with another patient, but you can lie down in the second consulting room. She'll be with you shortly. Travis, you want to help Katy down the hall? Second door on the left."

Katy nudged him and he moved automatically to follow Dora's directions. He didn't speak as he helped Katy onto the examination table, and then leaned against the opposite wall. Okay, so Dora hadn't reacted as he'd expected, but she was a trained nurse-cum-receptionist. She'd probably grown inured to seeing the ugly side of life.

The door was pushed wide and the doctor, a woman in her mid-thirties, entered the room. She offered him a quick smile before turning to her patient. "Hi, Katy. What have you done?"

"Lisa, hi. I fell on my behind fairly hard, and I think my coccyx is bruised. It hurts to sit and I had pain running down my legs when I walked a few steps."

"Did you hit your head when you fell?"

"I don't think so."

The doctor removed a small twig from Katy's hair and glanced at Travis. She raised an eyebrow. "Did you see her fall?"

"Yes. She fell on her bottom and kind of tumbled backwards head over heels. I thought she might have been concussed."

The doctor picked up a slim torch and checked Katy's pupils. "Normal pupil dilation and reaction. Did she lose consciousness at all?"

"No, but she looked shocky on the horse when I took her back to the house."

"So you were riding?" Lisa gently probed Katy's head.

"God, no! At least not when I fell. Afterwards, I rode."

Lisa frowned and Travis pitied her enough to translate. "I was on Mercury and Katy didn't like it when my horse stuck his head too close. She stepped back and slipped and took a tumble. Then I put her on Mercury's back to bring her home and I think she—Katy—freaked out."

"Ah, thank you. I'm going to examine you now. Can you unzip your jeans for me and then I'll roll you onto your side and have a look at the damage."

Katy's eyes widened and she glanced at Travis.

Doctor Manning's gaze travelled from Katy to him, and back to her patient. "Would you prefer your boyfriend to stay or go?"

"He's not my boyfriend."

"We're not dating."

Their responses ran over the top of one another and Travis pushed off the wall. Unsure which of them was more embarrassed, he yanked the door wide open. "I'll wait outside. In the hall."

Leaving the women to the examination he pulled the door closed behind him and leaned against the opposite wall. What the hell had he been thinking, taking so long to leave the room?

Lips made to kiss on the girl that I miss . . .

Of course, he hadn't been thinking. At least not about the situation. The riff played and he closed his eyes and let his mind wander, trying to recapture the moment when it had drifted into his consciousness. He changed the key signature and tried it again. Was it meant to be sad? Hopeful? Where was he that he was missing *his* girl? Digging into his pocket for a piece of paper and a pencil, familiar excitement thrummed through him. Post-accident and rehabilitation had consumed all his energy and all his attention until . . .

Until his muse returned in the guise of a dark-haired beauty who had blocked his path and demanded to speak to him. Now, he couldn't erase the image of her face, or the refrain about her lips. And he knew, come hell or high water, he'd agree to talk to her later if only to draw further inspiration from watching her.

Chapter Seven

Kookaburras cackled from the high branches of the gum trees along the back fence line. As Katy lay in bed the morning after her fall, it seemed the birds competed for the title of 'longest cackle', or 'cheeriest performer'. The thought drew a smile as she rolled onto her back and stretched, kicking the sheet off as she wriggled with the sheer pleasure of moving. Yesterday's fall had hurt and for a little while, despite what she'd told Travis, she'd been worried her tailbone had been damaged. Doctor Manning had reassured her. "It's only bruised, but sitting on a hard seat will be uncomfortable for the next few days."

She could live with bruising.

Sharp tapping like Morse code began on her window. She swung her legs over the side of the bed and sat up. A groan slipped out at the change of angle and the pressure on her coccyx killed her optimism. Gingerly she set her feet on the floor and eased to a standing position before taking a few steps to the closest window.

She pulled the curtains open and a flash of black and white flapped away. A magpie-lark landed on the washing line, its call telling her off in bird language as she looked out at the day. Fine and clear with not a wisp of cloud in the sky. And while the action of walking had made her aware of her bruised bottom, she *could* walk if she took it slowly. "Thank goodness for small mercies, Gran," she whispered to the rose bush around which Gran's ashes would eventually be spread. "Now I understand what you meant by that."

Banging started again at the creek-side window, louder and growing more frenzied. A memory tugged in her mind and she peeped around the side of the curtains. A second bundle of black and white feathers in the form of a female magpie-lark pecked at her window. Just so had the birds woken her each morning every Christmas holiday when their reflections incited their territorial posturing.

She could still hear Gran's voice telling her, 'It's their way of saying hello and welcome home, Katy.'

Home—yes, the magpie-larks were welcoming her to her home. She tapped on the window in response. "Hello to you too, Mrs Lark. It's good to be home." And it was.

Grabbing her summer robe off the hook behind the door and tying the sash in a bow, she headed for the kitchen. Or rather, she waddled like a duck. Dignified walking was probably out of the question for a few days. Setting the coffee pot to percolate on the gas top while she filled a saucepan with water to boil eggs, she thought about meeting Travis, his anger and closed-off attitude. Was that all to do with his scars? Neither Bessie nor Dora had seen him, and Geilis hadn't known of his return. Certainty filled her that he'd refused to answer the door when she visited the farmhouse, not that she'd missed him. The eye she'd imagined at the window hadn't been a reflection.

Sadness filled her that the singer she'd loved since her teens had become a recluse. Her skill set had grown since finishing her degree and in the time she'd been working as a carer, and both helped her understand the effects of loss. And while she struggled to make sense of her own personal losses, maybe she could help Travis back into the community and get him through the darkness that sat in his eyes.

She had just added two brown eggs to the boiling water when she heard a motorbike pull into her driveway and park beneath the kitchen window. She reached the window as the rider removed his helmet.

Travis!

She knew it was ridiculous to think her imagination had conjured him out of thin air. Nevertheless his arrival set her heart rate skipping with pleasure. She knocked on the window and, when he looked up, pointed towards the back door. By the time she reached for the lock and opened it, he was standing outside the door, hair all over the place and looking a lot less angry than yesterday. In fact, one side of his mouth pulled up in a half-smile as her gaze met his.

"Good morning. I hope I haven't caught you at a bad time." His gaze dropped briefly and she tugged the sides of her robe together as she remembered what she was wearing.

"No. Your timing is excellent. Coffee's just finished percolating if you'd like a cup."

"Ah, thanks. I just wanted to check you're okay."

"Aside from waddling like a duck you mean? No, I'm okay, but thanks for thinking of me. Can you grab a couple of mugs from that cupboard behind you please?" While his back was turned she made it to the stove, turned off the gas to both the coffee and her boiled eggs and left the latter to finish cooking in near-boiling water.

She poured coffee into both mugs and sat gingerly on the plump cushion in her usual chair, expecting Travis to take the one opposite facing the window. He hesitated for a moment and then moved to the chair at the end of the table, out of the bright morning light.

Angling his face a little to the left, he picked up the mug she passed to him and sipped his coffee. "That's a nice roast. Did you bring it with you from the city?"

She shook her head and sipped, tasting the new blend for the first time. "It's pretty good. No, I picked this up in Dalton a couple of days ago from a little café in the homeware centre. Do you know it?"

"I haven't been—shopping for a while. I get everything I need delivered."

"Oh. Well, you should pop in there one day. They have quite a variety for a small café."

He grunted, a noncommittal sound that tugged at her heart. "I'm glad you dropped in this morning. I want to thank you again for helping me yesterday."

"No problem. Mercury sends his regrets by the way."

"Mercury? Is that your horse's name?"

"Yep. You really were out of it yesterday, weren't you?"

"I've never been good with big animals. Give me a dog any day. Didn't you used to have a dog—his name started with a B, I think?"

"Bonzer, yeah. Long gone. He died not long after Dad passed away."

She nodded and sipped her coffee, building up the nerve to tell him about her idea. How would he react to the request to be a part of her campaign to win a spot on the renovation show, especially seeing how reluctant he was to see people? Was it stupid to think she could make a difference to their town? "Can I ask you something?"

His hand stopped in the act of raising his coffee and his eyes narrowed over the top of the mug. The word 'wary' would never have applied to Travis back when his career was taking off, but she couldn't think of any other way to describe his expression. "It's okay, you don't have to worry. I'm not going to ask you for an organ donation." She tried to inject a laugh into her comment but nerves turned it into a high-pitched giggle.

She cleared her throat and tried again, pitching her voice lower. "You were born in this town; I've only ever visited during school holidays. Coming back this time"—God, it was hard to think about this as a homecoming without Gran here to wrap her loving arms around Katy—"I've really noticed how depressed the town is. Have you any ideas what I could do, what I could contribute to bring people back to Lark Creek?"

Travis frowned and she felt as though she was speaking a foreign language. "What do you mean?"

"You see, I don't want to sell Gran's—my house, but—"

"Your house?" All of a sudden he sat up and looked around as though realising Gran's absence for the first time. "Where's Merle?"

"She passed away a couple of months ago. Didn't you know?"

***

Travis bent his head and his hand tightened on the mug. *How bloody self-absorbed had he been that he hadn't known his nearest neighbour had died?*

"Katy, I'm so sorry. I didn't know. What happened?"

"Bessie found her. She came looking when Gran didn't arrive for their walk. Apparently Gran had a massive stroke. No one was with her. She didn't have a chance." Katy blinked furiously and sniffed a couple of times before getting awkwardly to her feet and grabbing a couple of tissues from a box on the windowsill. "I should have been here. If I'd been here maybe she'd be alive today."

"Stop thinking like that." His words sounded harsh even to his own ears.

Katy froze, aside from her eyes. They blinked rapidly before she stared at him as though he'd gone mad. "Pardon?"

"That *if only* stuff will do your head in. Look, it changes nothing to imagine a different sequence of events, a different timing or a decision to do, or not to do something. If only I had taken the limo put on for me instead of riding my bike; if only I had been two seconds earlier or later to that intersection. If only the truck driver had driven to the weather conditions . . . No amount of wishing can change anything. You just have to live with how things are. And make the best of them."

Katy's gaze flicked away from his and he imagined it settling on his cheek. He could feel it like a weight pressing on his scarred flesh, and shame forced him to turn away. He was good at dispensing advice, but living by what he said?

"Is that what you're doing—making the best of how things are?" Her voice was soft, not accusing him as he deserved, but her words poked and pried into that shrivelled, most private place deep within him, the secret kernel of himself where he'd barricaded the door against everyone and refused to examine his decision to hide away.

Angry with himself for exposing even this small hint of how he felt, he pushed to his feet. "It's none of your business. I can see you're over your tumble so I'll be on my way." Cringing inwardly at his rudeness, still he strode through the door and away from Katy Leonard. She saw too much and her softness would be his undoing if he stayed. That gentle compassion might tempt him to imagine other things were possible.

And when she rejected the monster he was? That sort of scar he'd never overcome.

Chapter Eight

The increasing volume of a Nirvana song woke Katy from her heat-induced nana-nap and she reached for her phone as it vibrated its way across the cane table. Just why she'd assigned that ringtone to her sister, she wasn't sure, unless it was the certainty that echoed Rosie's reliability in every heavy beat. She stabbed the green button and closed her eyes. "Hi, Rosie, all set for your trip?"

"Katy? Have you heard from Adam today?" Rosie's voice sounded tight, breathless, as though the words were strangled as they tried to escape. They frightened Katy. Her eyes flew open and she sat up quickly, groaning as the pressure on her tailbone sent pain shooting up her back and down her legs.

With a determined heave, she stood. "I haven't heard from him. Why? What's happening?"

"He's disappeared. We're supposed to be leaving for Japan tonight and when I went to his room to check on his packing, he wasn't there. His guitar case is gone and I'm missing a hundred dollars from my wallet."

"That's—"

Worrying? Scary? Awful?

"What can I do? Do you want me to drive down to help look for him?"

"No, stay there. I'm hoping—I just wondered if you'd heard from him because—I was silly enough to mention your offer to Geoff in Adam's hearing."

It took Katy a few moments to remember what offer Rosie was referring to. "Do you think he might head out to see me?"

"It's possible. He doesn't lump you in with old fogey parents."

"What time are you supposed to fly out?"

"Ten o'clock tonight, but there's no way we're leaving without Adam."

An incoming message pinged on Katy's phone. "Hang on, Rosie. A message just arrived. Let me check who it's from." She took the phone from her ear and clicked into the inbox.

Hi Katy I'm on bus arriving Dalton 4 pm C U soon Adam

Relief surged through her, quickly joined by worry about her runaway nephew. "Rosie? Adam messaged me that he's on the bus heading out to visit me. What do you want me to do?"

A soft sob, quickly choked back, came over the line followed by her brother-in-law's voice. "Katy, it's Geoff. Thank God Adam had enough sense to message you. Look, are you okay with looking after him for the holidays? If not, say so. I'll come and fetch him and then book new flights for us tomorrow."

"It's fine, Geoff. If Adam's coming to me I'm happy to look after him until you get home." If her nephew had chosen to come to her, she would welcome him and care for him as Gran had looked after her. Because Rose Cottage was about family. And now it was her home.

"Thanks. We set up a home schooling account for him to finish off the school year. I'll send you the log in details and notify the school about the changes. We'll talk more later, but I'll transfer some funds into your account to pay for his keep."

It was as easy as that.

It might only be early November, but the spring sun beat down on Katy's head and shoulders as though summer had arrived. She ducked under the meagre shade of the bus shelter. Adam's bus should be arriving soon, but she had been pacing the footpath like an expectant father banished from the delivery suite. The Dalton town hall clock chimed the hour with a fussy series of notes far too formal for the setting. A minute had passed since she'd last looked at the time. A whole sixty seconds. How could sixty seconds drag so badly?

Smiling wryly, she thought how Rosie would think she was loopy, wanting, and at the same time worried about seeing her nephew. Closing her eyes, she tried to distract herself by imagining what would bring guests to her B & B—if she chose that alternative. There were a number of attractions in this part of the country for tourists.

The military museum . . . the zoo . . . a proposed unique species garden . . . All were worthy destinations, but nothing was close enough to include Lark Creek as a stopover unless the town had something of its own to offer. They needed a drawcard, more than the vineyard alone, something like an adventure park with outdoor activities to cater for kids to adults. A zip line would be pretty cool. A series of zip lines like she'd flown on in north Queensland would be even better.

Dream on, Katy-Kate. It was always Rosie's voice she heard in her head when she dreamed too big. Or when she took off on another *adventure.*

Once upon a time, before Dad died, she'd imagined travelling the world, going wherever fate took her. After Dad's death, that freedom to go anywhere had become a way to escape being too close to everyone. It had led to her missing out on a final visit with Gran. For that, she couldn't forgive herself.

Shuffling from the couple on her left drew her attention and she looked down the road. A Greyhound bus had turned the corner, its front windows dusty in the afternoon sun. Through the wiper-washed section in front of the driver, she saw movement in the front row. Was that Adam in the front seat? A fluttering of nerves dipped and soared like butterflies in her stomach. It would be good to spend time with him. It would be fun. If she told herself it would be fine often enough, she could make it reality. She liked her nephew—a lot—but being his guardian for two or three months . . .

Did Rosie truly think her little sister was responsible enough to take on that role?

Wiping sweaty palms on her shorts, she watched the bus door open with a hydraulic hiss. An elderly woman climbed slowly down the stairs and was hugged by the only other people waiting at the stop. Katy peered around the little knot of people blocking the door.

Where was Adam?

"Hey, are you Katy Leonard?" The bus driver called down the stairs and Katy nodded.

"Yes, I'm expecting my nephew. He's about fourteen and—"

"Look, love, he got me to drop him off at the homemaker centre on the outskirts of town. Said you were picking him up there and pointed out your car, but he gave me your name just in case he had it wrong."

Anxiety pinged in Katy's brain and the butterflies in her belly grew bigger. "Oh, okay. I didn't know there was a bus stop there. My sister didn't tell me where he was getting off. Thanks. I'll go there now."

The driver nodded and closed the door. With a squeaking of brakes being released, the bus departed and Katy stood nibbling her thumbnail as she watched the vehicle turn onto the main road.

She walked back to her car and gingerly lowered herself onto the seat. Even with a cushion for her bruised tailbone her back was sore and the numbing effect of painkillers had worn off. As she drove out of the parking space, a spasm ran down her leg, her foot jerked on the accelerator and she took off with a squealing of tyres that startled two crows feasting in the middle of the road. They flapped out of her way, cawing indignantly. "You don't have to explain to my sister why you weren't at the right stop to meet Adam off the bus," she said to the birds. Rosie wouldn't think much of Katy's ability to look after her nephew if she knew. Maybe she wouldn't mention the miscommunication.

She turned into the homemaker centre and drove slowly along the road in front of the shops. At the far end, a lanky figure slouched against a shopfront, a duffle bag and a guitar case at his feet. Slowing the car as she approached, relief surged through her when Adam looked up and gave her a half-hearted wave. He picked up his gear and loped across the road and slung the bags on her back seat before plumping into the passenger seat. "Hi, Katy."

"Hello, Adam, I'm so sorry I'm late. I was waiting at the

other bus stop. I didn't know there was another stop here."

"Yeah, no probs."

"I can park if you want to get a drink or anything?"

"Nah, all good. I grabbed a soft drink while I was waiting."

Injecting enthusiasm she was far from feeling into her voice, she smiled at him. "Great. I've bought loads of food and I'll cook a really nice dinner for you tonight. What's your favourite meal?"

"Spaghetti Bolognese with loads of parmesan on it."

She'd bought mince and tomatoes on the strength of meals she remembered from visits with Rosie. Tick one item off her list for Adam's visit. "Consider it done."

"I didn't know there was another bus stop and I'm really sorry, but he's fine, honestly." Katy clutched her phone and stared out into a nearly moonless night. The fine sliver of new moon hung like a piece of lemon peel in the western sky. Fireflies danced down near the creek bank and the nightly cicada chorus ramped up another decibel as she waited for her sister's reaction. When it came down to it, she hadn't been able not to tell her sister about the arrival mishap.

Rosie's sigh was soft, but Katy heard it and cringed. "He's fine so it isn't an issue. Just—"

"I'll take good care of him, I promise. I won't let him get into any trouble. There's nowhere for him to get into trouble here anyway."

"I appreciate you looking after him, Katy-Kate. After Mum remarried and we spent all those holidays at Lark Creek with Gran, we swore we'd never palm our children off onto family members, yet here I am, about to fly off to Japan."

"Rosie, your research is important. It's not the same as Mum shunting us off to Gran's. And it's a one-off, not a lifestyle choice. Adam knows you love him and besides, he'll get a taste of what your teen years were like out here."

"Thanks, little sis." In the background down the line she heard Rosie's husband speaking. "Got to go. Geoff said our taxi's here—Love you."

"You too. Safe travels." She ended the call and sat listening to the sounds of the country. It was so different to her little rented apartment in Brisbane. Out here there was room to move, but she was lonely. Most of her friends were back on the coast. Other than Geilis, there hadn't been many kids of her age in Lark Creek. Rosie had done better and cultivated a couple of friendships, but at ten years older than Katy, she'd been more adult and maybe—Katy conceded reluctantly—wiser. Aside from Bessie up the road and Geilis, who did she really know?

That was going to change. If she was going to set up Gran's home as a B & B, she'd need to know the people in town much better. And maybe, if the television thing worked out, the reno show might bring much-needed attention to Lark Creek, and she'd make a permanent place for herself.

A board creaked in the house and she turned her head to see if Adam was coming to join her. He'd been quiet over dinner and shut himself into his bedroom as soon as it was finished with little more than a curt 'gonna ring a mate' before he disappeared.

Katy knew what missing your school friends was like, and holidays sucked even worse when Rosie went to university and left her little sister to fend for herself. "Adam? Do you want a mug of cocoa?"

There was no reply, and when she walked down the hall, no light showed beneath his door. She tapped and waited, but a murmur suggested he might be on the phone to his mate and she was loath to intrude on his first night. Sighing, she picked up her laptop. With responsibility for Adam, but no company for the evening, she might as well settle in and research what attractions in their area came up on a Google search. Then she could tick off another item on her list.

The thought of actually finishing something for the first time in months felt surprisingly good.

Chapter Nine

Travis slowed the quad bike as he came off the hill and passed through the last gate into the main yard, a trailer full of deadfall wood hooked on behind. Expeditions such as this one had been in the company of his father when he was alive. Gems of paternal wisdom filtered into his mind at odd times, like now. Observations mostly to do with living on the land, which Travis had let flow in one ear and out the other. Or so he'd thought.

Clearly some things had stuck because this morning, he'd looked at the weather forecast and current fire warning and his father's voice had spoken in his head, softly, but so clear he could have been in the next room.

No point feeding a bushfire, is there, son?

And Travis had jumped on the quad straight after breakfast and headed out to the far paddock and begun collecting fallen wood.

As he ran down the rutted track towards the smallest of three sheds, a figure—he couldn't tell if it was male or female from this distance—disappeared into the trees lining the back fence. Annoyance licked at the trespass and a muscle ticked in his cheek.

But it was nothing compared to the anger that welled as he drove past the house and caught sight of the side of the barn. Vivid angry swirls of colour sat over slashes of black . . . and in the bottom right hand corner there was a tag.

"Shit. What the hell—" Graffiti with an indecipherable tag.

On his barn.

In the back of beyond.

Casting a single look at the spot where the lone figure had vanished into the trees, Travis turned off the quad engine, dug out the key for his motorbike and strode into the shed. "Whoever you are, you'll pay for this." He tossed off the tarp covering his new Harley and swung his leg over the seat. Revving the engine, he tore out of the shed and down the back paddock. Before the day was over he'd weld the damned gate shut and begin to throw up a barrier bigger than even Trump's proposed southern wall. Two incursions in the same week was beyond trespassing. It was a downright invasion and no one invaded his privacy. No one.

***

Katy looked through the lounge room window in surprise as a familiar motorbike pulled up on the grass verge in front of Rose Cottage. The fanciful name had been given by Gran back when she arrived as a young bride with ideas of roses around the front gate. And there were roses—run wild, with long thorny stems hanging low to catch the unwary. Mentally adding *trim the roses* to her epic to-do list, she opened the front door.

A tall figure in dirt-streaked denims, a plaid shirt and sporting a helmet as the only concession to road safety climbed off the motorbike. He removed his helmet, pushed open the gate and strode up the path towards her. She stepped through the doorway and crossed the wide veranda. Travis had left in a temper yesterday. She'd touched a raw nerve, of that she was certain. But it wasn't her problem; it wasn't her fault if he was touchy about how things had turned out for him. He was the one who'd raised the topic of making the best of what you had.

Hazel eyes glared at her and she stopped halfway down the stairs. One foot hovered over the edge ready to take the next step, but that glare held her back. Why was he here if he wasn't happy to see her?

Some perverse sense of self-preservation flickered to life within her. Gran had lived her life by the motto, *smile and the world smiles with you.* In Gran's house, Katy would try to keep her spirit alive by applying the same principles. She smiled at her visitor in the hope he would rethink whatever was making him annoyed. "Good morning. Lovely day, isn't it?"

"Where is he?"

"Who?" Her throat felt as though it was closing. The only 'he' in the house was Adam. Surely he couldn't have got into trouble

50

already. Not in the three hours since he'd got out of bed and grunted at her request to help move furniture in the shed so she could see what Gran had stored in there. Wishing she had a barking dog to deter whatever was coming next, she cleared her throat. "Why do you want to see—the 'he' who lives here?"

Travis' eyes narrowed and he examined the house behind her. "How old is he?"

"I don't see what business it is of yours. Why don't you—"

"He's vandalised my barn. I want him to fix it."

Words clogged in her throat and her legs felt less stable than a bowl of jelly.

Please no.

She cleared her throat and gripped the handrail. "That's not possible. He's been here all morning, doing his schoolwork." At least she was reasonably sure Adam had been inside. For a while she'd heard him stomping around as she attempted to clear a path between the stuff stacked in the shed before she popped her ear buds in and turned up the volume of her music. "You'll see. I'll call him out and you can ask him yourself. Adam, come out here please."

She waited without hearing signs of her nephew and turned to Travis. "I'll be back in a moment. He's probably listening to his music and can't hear me." A sound like a snort emerged from behind her as she climbed the stairs. As she approached Adam's bedroom and knocked on his door, she held her breath.

Please don't let him have done anything wrong. Please don't let him start off on the wrong foot.

"What?" Fourteen-year-old narkiness greeted her as she opened the door.

Firming her resolve, she took a deep breath and injected as much of her sister's parent tone into her voice as she could. "Adam, there's someone asking for you out the front. Come out now please."

"I'm busy. I'm—doing my schoolwork."

"Too bad. You have a visitor. Put your laptop away and come now."

An exaggerated sigh, a carefully casual tossing of the laptop onto the bed, and Adam slouched across the room and pushed past her. He shoved his hands in the pockets of his cargo shorts and the waist slipped even lower, exposing more than the waistband of his underpants.

Katy rolled her eyes and followed Adam onto the veranda and waited at the top of the steps as he eyed off Travis. "Yeah, what d'ya want?"

"That graffiti you sprayed on the side of my barn—you're going to scrub it off."

Katy gasped, but it was nothing to her shock when she looked at Adam. His cheeks paled, and then turned a dull red. "Not me. I haven't been out this morning."

"So you're telling me there are two young people dressed identically in khaki cargo pants and a black T-shirt wandering in the vicinity of my shed this morning?"

"Adam?" Wildly praying Travis had the wrong house, the wrong teenager, Katy came down a couple of steps and put her arm around Adam's shoulders. "Did you go out this morning? Did you graffiti Travis' barn?"

She heard and saw the nervous swallow, the bobbing up and down of his Adam's apple and her heart sank. The when and the how didn't matter. He'd done it and he'd been caught out, and by God, she'd make sure he made restitution somehow.

"Why do you believe this bloke and not me?"

Before she had a chance to wonder how Rosie would handle the situation, Travis replied, "Maybe because you're wearing the same colours sprayed on my barn in your hair."

Katy blinked and looked at Adam. Hair stuck up in spikes because of course he hadn't brushed it. "I can't see—"

"On the other side." Travis pointed at the right side of Adam's head.

Katy pulled his shoulder until he faced her. How had she missed seeing the bright yellow paint in his hair? And the black between his right thumb and fingers before he hastily shoved his hand back into his pocket. Her stomach clenched, she dragged in a breath and wildly wondered if Rosie knew about Adam's latest interest. "Too late to hide. How could you, Adam?"

"So, I'll take him back with me and he can make a start on cleaning up the mess he made."

"Take him back? Hold on a sec, I'm not letting him go anywhere with anyone, regardless of the evidence of his guilt. I'm responsible for him; I'll bring him."

Travis folded his arms over his chest and glared at her again. He huffed out an audible breath that carried a degree of frustration with it.

But all he had to worry about was a shed with a bit of paint over it whereas she had a teenager with attitude and no idea how to deal with him. Adam hadn't come with an instruction manual, and why hadn't Rosie forewarned her of potential problems?

'*He's good with paint.*' Katy had taken Rosie's throwaway comment before she boarded the plane to mean Adam would be good with a paint brush. On a wall chosen by her in a colour to match the rest of Gran's interior. Not with a spray can adding his tag to a neighbour's wall.

Anger, frustration, worry—whirled inside Katy's mind as she met Travis' steady gaze. "Look, I believe you, but I need to see the extent of the damage he's caused, and I need to stay with him while he works. He's my nephew and my responsibility."

"Fair enough. I'll expect a decent start made on cleaning off the graffiti in the morning. But don't expect me to hang around while he cleans it off. I've better things to do with my time than supervise a delinquent adolescent." He stalked off and moments later, the motorbike roared through a gate in the lower corner of Thornyhill and up the back paddock until the sound was lost over the far side of the hill.

Adam slouched against the railing, hands deep in his pockets, lower lip pushed out in a mutinous, monumental sulk. "Why should I clean his shed? It's not like I didn't make it look better. I don't really have to go, do I?"

Katy ran a hand through her hair and slowly climbed the stairs. Day one of Adam's visit had barely begun and he'd already alienated her neighbour. If she let her nephew get away with this, soon he'd think he could graffiti any building in town and then what would happen to her plans for the B & B? And what would happen to her ability to care for him if he didn't respect her and the boundaries she knew she had to set?

She turned to face him and thought hard before she spoke. "What you did was wrong and now you have to fix it. I'll come with you, but you'll do the clean up. And you'll need to think about the apology you're going to make to Mr Roberts."

"No way!"

"Yes, way. After that's been sorted we'll talk about expectations and—and goals, and stuff like that." Which meant she'd better start planning so she sounded like she had a clue what she was talking about. Maybe this was why Rosie made lists for everything in her life. Maybe list-making was how *adulting* got done. Hoping like hell it was the answer to her dilemma, she led the way inside with the promise of another of Adam's favourite meals for tonight's dinner.

Chapter Ten

Travis parted the gap in the curtains and eyed the boy's progress. Make that *lack of progress*. He'd been scrubbing the same panel for fifteen minutes and as far as Travis could see, the paint hadn't noticeably decreased.

Damn it. The side of the barn would need repainting to get rid of the boy's vandalism. Two top coats at least.

He gritted his teeth and looked at Adam's aunt—God, it was hard to think of Katy of the lush lips in such terms. She leaned one knee on the bale of hay he'd intended to mulch the newly-turned herb garden with. Glossy black hair was pulled into a high ponytail that swung with a life of its own as she tipped her head to one side, then the other and gave her attention to a piece of paper in her hand. As he watched, she applied a pen to the paper, bit her bottom lip and looked towards the house. His heart thudded as though it would break through his chest. Thudded with fear she'd not forgive him for his damnable outburst in her kitchen.

Why had he lashed out like that?

He glanced at his watch. Damn and double damn. He should have been up earlier, but the pain medication he'd taken last night had made him drowsy and he'd slept through the alarm. Sleeping in might be a luxury—sometimes—but today it had trapped him inside his own home. His right hand shook as he parted the curtains and glared through the window again—Adam wasn't going to be finished anytime soon.

And he wasn't prepared to face Katy—not yet. Pushing his hand's capability yesterday had felt like a step in the right direction. If he didn't use his hand, it seized up. If he overused it . . . He grimaced at the notion of facing anyone. Not while his hand was shaking like the wheels of an out-of-control Harley. But unless he did something he'd be trapped in his house until Katy realised how impossible it was to scrub paint off the shed.

He pulled out his mobile and scrolled through until he found her phone number. Glancing through the window, his thumb hovered over the blue digits as Katy stretched her arms to the sky. The movement raised her cut-off top and bared an expanse of skin above short shorts and a pair of tanned and toned legs. His mouth dried and he parted the curtain a little more. Did she know he was there? Was that little performance for his benefit because she had realised the futility of further scrubbing?

Maybe he *was* becoming the grumpy bastard Kyle had called him, but Ms Leonard was too attractive for her own good and he refused to allow that to distract him from his course of action. Her nephew had vandalised his property and someone had to pay to fix the damage.

She crossed to stand beside her nephew and they took a few steps back and looked at the panel the boy had been scrubbing before turning to look at the untouched section of the shed. He imagined their conversation coming to the same conclusion he'd reached.

"Yeah, you want to factor in a few litres of undercoat plus top coat, 'cos washing won't do a damned thing." As though she'd heard him, Katy turned and looked at the house and suddenly he got a sinking feeling in his gut. She spoke over her shoulder to the boy before strolling towards the house.

"I knew it." Travis let go of the curtain, looked at Katy's phone number and hit the call button as he raced for the front door and turned the lock. Heart beating faster than it should, he slipped into the study and flattened himself against the wall beside the window. She had a foot on the bottom tread when he heard a familiar piece of music.

Her ringtone was the chorus of his last hit?

Blinking at the absurdity of the situation, he watched as she fumbled the phone out of her pocket and cast an embarrassed glance at the house before answering the call. If it hadn't been such a near thing he'd have laughed aloud.

"Katy Leonard. Who's calling?" Her voice was upbeat and slightly breathless. *Because of having his music as her ringtone when she stood on his front steps?*

"Katy, Travis Roberts here."

"Oh, hi. I guess you aren't at home then?"

"No. I'm calling to find out if your nephew has finished cleaning my shed yet?"

"About that." She glanced at his house and her tongue swept across her top lip. That breathless quality returned to her voice. "It isn't coming off very well. I'm not sure what to do about it."

"What do you mean, *not very well*? Either it's coming off or it's not. Which is it?"

"Um, not, I guess. Adam's been scrubbing for ages, but—"

"So if it won't wash off, he can paint over it."

"Of course, yes, do you have paint for the shed? He can start now if you tell me where to find it."

"You aren't suggesting I pay for paint to cover graffiti your nephew sprayed on my wall, are you?"

"Oh. . . I . . .oh, I didn't think of that. Look, can I call in and talk to you when you get home? Hopefully we can work something out."

"I'm not interested in talking about it. Either your nephew begins repainting my shed tomorrow morning, or tomorrow afternoon, you'll be hearing from my solicitor. I haven't called the police yet, but—"

"Please don't call the police. I'll organise whatever needs to be done." Her voice rose, high and pleading, and he felt a tug of guilt at pushing her on it. It was just a shed, and painting over the damage would be more of an inconvenience to him. Did it really matter?

"I don't know where he got the spray cans, but his mother would kill him if he got into trouble out here. She'll probably kill me for not taking better care of him, but—"

Something snapped in his memory, and the face of his best friend from school flittered back through the years. Rick had no one to care about him, to pull him up when he did something stupid and put him back on the right path. Not like Travis' parents. If only someone had bothered to give Rick some tough love, he might not have ended up in jail. Travis refused to let another young man go down that road for want of sufficient guidance, which Katy seemed to have difficulty providing.

Injecting sternness into his tone, Travis cut her off. "He's done wrong and caused property damage. He needs to learn that he can't get away with committing a crime."

"I agree with you. It's just that—"

"No excuses. He has until tomorrow afternoon to begin rectifying his delinquent actions. After that, I'll call the police. Good day."

Chapter Eleven

Dumbstruck by Travis Roberts' demand, Katy took Adam back to Rose Cottage. She wanted to rail at her neighbour's hard line stance and tell him where he could stuff his attitude. But deep down, she knew he was right. Rosie would have already made the offer to repaint his shed because Rosie was the responsible sister. But Rosie wasn't going to learn of her son's behaviour because she would be upset with him and disappointed that her irresponsible, flighty little sister had lived up to her reputation. Or was that *down* to it? It sucked being treated like the baby of the family even though she was, and it sucked that nobody thought she was capable of doing anything important or significant. Like looking after her nephew. Or transforming Gran's home into a beautiful B & B.

Dad had believed in her, and Gran.

But somewhere inside her the person they'd seen and believed in still lived—strong, resilient, capable. Shaking her head, it occurred to Katy maybe her father had believed in the power of self-fulfilment. He said he believed, and she would achieve. Nobody else thought she could. And Gran? Gran had wrapped her in love, accepting Katy as she was.

Since Dad's death, Katy had been on the move. Avoiding staying in one place more than a few months by picking up casual work had felt liberating—although Rosie called it something else. 'Failure to settle down with a permanent job is immature, Katy. Grow up and get a real job. Contribute something to society.'

Now she had a chance to do something good. Something positive and beautiful. She would turn Rose Cottage into a desirable B & B and find a way to attract tourists to Lark Creek. Just as soon as she worked out how she was going to pay for paint to fix Adam's vandalism.

Leaning back in Gran's seat on the veranda, she stared at her laptop screen while rain fell in heavy drops, releasing perfumes of lavender and rosemary and something lemony she'd couldn't name. The night closed in as she Googled what she needed. Did paint really cost that much? If she didn't win a spot on that renovation show, there was no way she'd be able to afford to do up Gran's house. The paint alone would cost more than she had in her bank account. But before she could begin work on Rose Cottage, the owner of Thornyhill had to be satisfied.

"Katy?"

Startled by the intrusion of an unexpected voice, she looked up. Adam stood in the doorway, hands in their familiar position deep in the pockets of his cargo pants. "What's up, Adam?"

"Will that man really call the police to take me away?" The dim outside light cast his face into shadow, but his voice cracked on the question. He was young and worried, and her heart went out to him.

"No. I won't let him. We'll work it out somehow."

"I took some of Mum's money to pay for the bus ticket. After I bought my ticket I had fifty dollars when I got on the bus. I've only got ten left, but you can have that to put towards paint for that man's shed."

"In one day? What on earth did you spend forty—" Adam turned a dull red that even the low light and the night couldn't hide and Katy *knew*. "I see. The home ware centre wasn't meant to be your stop, was it? That's where you bought the spray cans."

His shoulders hunched higher and his gaze fixed firmly on the floorboards. "I didn't want to leave my mates and be stuck in Japan with my parents for the holidays. I wanted to have some fun so I came to you. I saw the centre and remembered my mate saying the only positive thing about the country was all the walls I could claim."

"What do you mean *claim*?"

"Paint and tag." Adam looked downright miserable and she was reminded that only last year, he'd been shorter than her and a mad keen cricketer and guitarist.

"I guess being stuck in the sticks might feel like a

punishment?"

"Yeah, it sucks. Oh, sorry, Kate. I don't mean you suck. It's just—"

"It's okay, Adam. I know what you mean. But here's the thing. You have a chance to fix the situation if we can work out a way to pay for the paint."

"Don't you have enough money to buy it?"

Heat rose in Katy's cheeks, but if she was going to set a good example for her nephew, honesty was the only option. "Your parents are going to deposit some money to help pay for groceries and stuff while you're here, but it's not in my account yet. So here's my plan. Tell me what you think of it."

Chapter Twelve

Adam was sitting at the table shoving spoonfuls of cereal into his mouth. He barely glanced up as she entered the room, but as she reached up to lift Gran's cast iron pan from the ceiling hook, a soft grunt escaped.

Adam peered up sideways. "What's up?"

She guessed his taciturnity was due to his age. And maybe a bit of embarrassment still lingered after Travis' visit, but she wasn't sure. At ten or twelve years of age, she'd have been certain of it, but now, it felt like she didn't know this adolescent version of Adam.

"I had a fall and hurt my tailbone, plus a few bruises into the bargain."

"Is that why you lie down during the day?"

She set the pan on the gas stove top and turned on the heat. "Yes. Nice to know you noticed. Do you want bacon and eggs after your cereal?"

Muffled by a mouthful of muesli, his "Yeah" was what she expected. But not what followed. He jumped up from the table, which sent his chair flying into the cupboard behind and strode to the fridge. He pulled out a packet of bacon and the box of eggs and brought them to where she stood, mouth open in surprise, in front of the stove. Adam hadn't done a single thing willingly since he'd arrived.

"Thanks. Um, how many eggs?"

"Two—uh, can I have three?"

"Sure, no problem. Gran's chooks are laying so well I thought I'd make a cake later. What sort do you like?"

He shrugged, that one-shouldered careless shrug that was his response to almost every question. But then his glance flicked up and met hers briefly. "I like chocolate. Mum makes great chocolate cake."

"Do you miss your mum and dad?" She hadn't factored homesickness into the equation, but maybe at fourteen, some of

Adam's behaviour was still just plain old missing his family.

"Nah . . . maybe a bit. Katy?"

"What's up?" She layered in several rashers and her mouth watered as the aroma of frying bacon wafted from the pan. Her stomach gurgled, which drew a chuckle from Adam.

"I'm guessing that's not all for me."

"Not on your life, mate."

He stood beside her, shuffling his bare feet on Gran's faded lino floor. "I'm sorry for stuffing up."

She flipped the bacon, turned on the heat for the second burner and cracked four eggs into the pan. "Thanks. But you know, it's easy to apologise. Words are meaningless without action. If you mean it, then show me."

"I'm going to paint the old guy's shed. Isn't that showing I mean it?"

Old guy? "Travis Roberts isn't old, Adam. Why he's probably only thirty-one or two."

"That's more than twice my age. That's ancient."

Stunned by Adam's perspective, she realised that in his world, over thirty was impossible to imagine. "Okay, so what does twenty-five make me? Merely old?"

"Aww, Katy, I didn't mean—"

She patted his shoulder. "Just teasing you. Okay, so painting Mr Roberts' shed is a good beginning and that's showing him you're sorry for the graffiti on his shed. Now you have to show me you mean what you say."

He frowned and threw himself onto a chair. It had probably been forty or more years since Gran's chairs had been subjected to the unco-ordinated strength of a teenage boy and the wood creaked in protest. "Honest, Katy, I got no idea what you want from me."

She flipped the eggs and turned off the gas to both burners before serving up breakfast. As she sat carefully on a cushion on the chair across from Adam, she commiserated with her nephew. Would her plan work, or was she going about dealing with Adam all wrong?

It might only be six years since she'd been a teenager, but everything she thought she knew about the species had flown out the window when she took on guardianship of Adam. "Well, you admit you stuffed up and that's a positive thing. But your actions created a difficult situation for me with our neighbour and fixing that relationship is going to be tricky until I can at least walk like a human and not like a duck."

"Why are you walking like a duck—oh, right. You fell over. Why's that a problem again?"

Katy sighed and picked up her cutlery and cut into her bacon. "Because even if I manage to drive you to the shop to buy paint, I can't see myself sitting for several hours on the ground beside Mr Roberts' shed while you undercoat it. It's just not going to happen today and maybe not tomorrow. The drive into Dalton to pick you up put my back into a spasm and I need to rest it for the day. And I can't let you go up there by yourself either, so we have a problem."

Adam's face paled and his knife clattered onto his plate. "You don't reckon he'll call the police when we don't turn up at his place, do you? He wouldn't, would he? But you're injured. He knows that, right?"

"Calm down, Adam, I'm sure he won't do anything drastic today."

The hunted look disappeared, but Adam still looked troubled.

"You know what? I'll give him a call, right after we've polished off breakfast and a cuppa. How's that?"

He nodded and dived back into his food, beating Katy by one mouthful to clear his plate.

Chapter Thirteen

Travis reached Mercury's withers with the currycomb as the phone rang. He pulled it out of his pocket with his left hand and checked the caller ID. A good night's sleep had changed his perspective. Determined not to be such an arrogant prick, he tried to inject some enthusiasm into his voice. "Hello, Katy."

"Hi." Was she hesitant because she had been prepared for more of the crap he'd dished up in that last phone call? Ashamed of himself, he thought about apologising, but it was something he needed to do face to face. And so he asked, "How are you feeling this morning?"

"Not too bad if I lie down, but sitting is a bit of a pain. Literally. That's what I wanted to talk about."

He stopped currying Mercury and frowned. "You wanted to talk about sitting?"

"Not exactly although it's all connected. About your shed—"

"That's got nothing to do with your injury." He was disappointed. Katy hadn't struck him as the type to welsh on a debt. She was soft on her nephew; that much he'd seen straight away, but she'd still brought him over to Thornyhill to make good on his vandalism. But trying to use her injury to get out of fixing the damage? Didn't she realise that kids needed boundaries, that without them they went off the rails. Rick Peyton, his old school friend, was a prime example.

"Well actually, it has. Driving Adam to the shop in Dalton to buy paint will be difficult; the local store doesn't have what we need, and I'm pretty sure I'm not able to sit around watching the paint dry while he works. Adam was anxious that you would call the police if we didn't turn up so I said I'd call you and explain our problem."

Like a smack on the head, Travis realised he'd jumped to a conclusion again—a totally wrong conclusion. What was wrong with him that he couldn't see beyond his own little world and empathise with Katy? He'd seen how much pain she was in when she sat in his car for the short ride to the doctor. Shame filled him. He'd never been such a self-centred bastard before his accident.

Had he?

"I'm sorry. I didn't think of that and I should have. Tell Adam not to worry about painting the shed until you're—I was going to say back on your feet, but that's not the problem."

She laughed, the sound rich and smooth as honey on warm toast. It reached past his shame and tugged at his recently revived memory of a teenage Katy at his going-away concert. She had been vivacious and her bright-eyed adoration when she asked for his autograph had given him a buzz. Like her laugh did now. It was the kind of laugh that led a man to forget himself and do silly things. Like compose a song to her lips.

"Got that right. So, you're okay with the postponement? And that's all it is. Adam will make good on fixing the damage. I promise you that."

"It's fine. And you were right to call me. I hadn't thought how your fall would affect Adam. Is there anything you need?" The words tumbled out unheeding of his plan not to go into town at all. But no matter how much the idea of confronting townsfolk and shop assistants made his stomach heave and his lungs squeeze, he couldn't snatch his words back. And oddly enough, he didn't want to if it meant helping Katy, and making up for his boof-headedness. Holding his breath he waited.

"Are you offering to pick up—stuff?"

Anxiety all but choked him. He swallowed nervously and made two attempts before he managed to speak around the lump in his throat. "Yeah, I guess I am. What do you need?"

"Hmm, well, I'd love to take advantage of your offer . . ."

Dry-mouthed and nauseous, Travis' heart thumped nineteen to the dozen. Who would he have to see? Could he just order what she needed online and have it delivered?

"But I went shopping the day I picked Adam up. Thanks

though. I really appreciate it."

"Anytime." He ended the call and rested his head against Mercury's neck. She didn't need anything and he felt giddy with relief. So giddy he'd tossed out another open offer.

Anytime? Did he really mean that or was it merely that his near miss made him casual with the truth? Securing the strap of the currycomb across his scarred hand, he resumed currying Mercury. For what it was worth, he reminded himself he'd already been into Lark Creek with Katy. While there had been a few curious looks, neither Dora or Dr Manning, nor the chemist at the pharmacy had reacted as he'd expected. Nobody had commented or offered fake sympathy. He hated sympathy. Hated the attention it focused on his scars and the way it brought back the night it happened.

Patting Mercury's neck, he tried to appreciate the fact he'd come out of the accident alive. Another inch and the huge wheel would have crushed him as he and his motorbike slid under the oil tanker on the wet road. A metal strut had sliced his hand and his cheek, but he'd walked away from the crash with his life. And it was worth living even if he couldn't play his guitar the way he used to. His damaged hand shook and he slid it out of the currycomb and fisted it. Breathing deeply, he blinked until the image of the underside of the truck faded.

It was time he got over himself and eased back into his hometown, into his community. He might not be able to play well enough to perform—but his brain was functioning. He could still create the music in his head; still earn a living by doing one of the things he loved. And if someone else got to play his music . . .

A pang of sadness for that part of him lost in the accident threatened to undermine this new and fragile optimism. He walked out of the barn into the sunshine and strolled to the edge of the incline. Below, the back paddock stretched away, uncultivated and gone to seed. He could buy a cow or a couple of goats and put them in the paddock to keep the grass down while he got back into composing.

Yesterday's riff played in his brain, insistent and beautiful, and drew him to his study. It was past time to get back to work. Katy's song beckoned.

***

Katy's finger hovered over the enter button before nerves got the better of her and she scrolled back for yet one more read through the application form. There had been nothing else she could add on the previous pass and yet, so much was riding on her success, she was reluctant to submit the form. At least while it was in her possession she could hope. And dream.

She looked across Gran's garden towards the creek. When she'd visited as a child, the water had flowed over the rocks with a gurgling sound that soothed her to sleep. Now, the sound of water trickling over rocks was soft and the water level was the lowest she'd ever seen it. There wasn't anything she could do about the lack of water, but Gran's home could be her home if she was able to convert it into a source of income. If she could win a spot on the renovation show and if she didn't dwell on the lack of a drawcard destination near Lark Creek, her dream was possible.

Before she could change her mind again she pressed the button and sent her application on its way. "And now, we wait."

"Who are you talking to?" Adam wandered onto the veranda, hands in pockets as though they were glued there, and threw himself onto a rickety cane chair. With a crack and a puff of dust, he fell through the seat. Eyes wide and mouth agog, he hung suspended, legs poking out at right angles.

Katy struggled to her feet and tottered towards him. Leaning on the intact arm of the chair, she held out her other hand. "Adam, give me your hand."

Adam wriggled and grunted, but his arms remained locked to his sides within the cane rim of the chair. "I can't get my hands out of my pockets. They're stuck. Katy—I'm stuck." His voice rose and Katy felt a fluttering of panic. At fourteen, Adam was already a couple of inches taller than her, even if he was still a string bean according to his father. If he couldn't get a hand out, how was she going to free him from the chair?

"Wait on, let me try from behind." With decreasing hope, she edged behind the chair. The space was too narrow to gain leverage and when she put her bottom against the railing and tried to push the chair forwards, her injured tailbone complained and shot pains down her leg.

Eventually she gave up trying. "We need muscle. I'll phone—" Who could she phone? Bessie? Could they free Adam between the two of them? Unbidden, an image of Travis on his horse flitted through her mind. He'd looked so powerful, like a giant riding out of the sun.

Anytime. He'd offered help and even though she knew he'd been referring to picking up groceries and the like, Adam's predicament qualified. She grabbed her phone and scrolled through until she found Travis' number. "The number of times we've phoned each other in the past couple of days, I should put him on speed dial. You okay, Adam?"

He looked anything but okay. "Terrific."

"We'll have you out of there real soon. Promise." But Katy became less sure as the number of rings increased. She had no idea who else she could call if—

"Hello?" Travis sounded distracted and definitely not welcoming, but just hearing his voice made her feel better.

"Travis, it's Katy. I'm sorry to bother you, but Adam's stuck in a chair and I can't pull him out. Can you come over and help please?" Silence greeted her request. "Travis, are you there?"

"I'm here. I'm just trying to work out what you meant. I thought you said Adam was stuck in a chair, but that doesn't make sense. Tell me again what's wrong."

"That's what I said. Adam fell through an old cane chair, his arms are pinned against his body and I can't get him out."

"Right, I'm coming over."

A few minutes later, the roar of a powerful motorbike engine shattered the quiet afternoon and quickly grew louder.

"He's coming through the paddock, Adam. Travis will have you out of there in no time."

Adam didn't look thrilled. "He'll think I'm an idiot. I look like an idiot stuck in this stupid chair. Why didn't you throw it out?"

Grumpy teenage angst and the fear of looking stupid—Katy remembered the emotions well. "I will once you're out of it, but some of Gran's possessions are old and frankly, Adam, I don't have the money to replace anything yet." She turned and moved to the top of the steps as Travis' motorbike passed the side fence and turned the front corner.

Travis pulled up on the grass verge beside the front gate and toed the kickstand into position before climbing off. He stood beside the bike, hands hanging loosely by his side and glanced up. What was he waiting for? Katy watched his hands curl into fists and he looked at the ground. Slowly he raised his hands and removed his helmet, as though the weight of it was almost more than he could bear. He hung it on the handlebar with careful deliberation, put his shoulders back and strode through the gate and up the stairs. His gaze roamed her face, heating her cheeks and sending legions of butterflies dancing in her tummy before he zeroed in on Adam.

"Now I get what you were saying." He stopped in front of Adam and eyed his predicament. "Okay, mate, I'm going to set you on your feet and then pull the chair off your backside. Ready?"

Adam nodded. "Yeah, ready."

Carefully, Travis tipped Adam and the chair and set him on his feet. "Katy, can you support Adam's shoulders and keep him balanced while I pull?"

"Of course." She moved into position. The rounded cane top pushed into her stomach as she reached beneath it and held Adam's shoulders.

"Okay, on the count of three." Travis set one booted foot against Adam's behind and gripped the outer rim of the seat while Katy braced herself. "One, two, three . . . "

Adam popped out like a cork from a champagne bottle and fell onto his knees. Katy grabbed the upright post to prevent herself doing the same. Travis leaned against the far railing holding the distorted skeleton of the cane chair aloft.

Embarrassed relief flooded Adam's face with colour as he scrambled to his feet. He stared at his rescuer and his eyes widened, but he managed to offer a stuttered "Thanks."

And it occurred to Katy that was how she must have looked at Travis. Her first close up look at his face had been a shock, but she'd known what he looked like before his accident. The scar running down his cheek didn't belong to that memory. Today she'd known what to expect and had barely noticed it, but Adam had probably been overwhelmed by guilt and fear and hadn't registered Travis' appearance at their first meeting. And—typical Travis—even angry as he'd been that day, he'd turned his face away.

"Are you okay?" Travis angled his head a little to the left. Once again she wondered if that movement was to hide his scar. The idea wasn't crazy; and it explained his odd behaviour. He looked from Katy to Adam and she wasn't sure which of them his question was intended for. When Adam didn't answer, she met Travis' gaze. "I'm fine. Adam, are you hurt?"

"Nah, all good." Hands on his lower back he stretched, but his gaze went back to Travis. "I'm gonna get a drink. Um, d'you want one, Mr Roberts?"

"Sure, thanks. Something cold." Adam left and Travis held up the remains of the chair. "Where's your bin? Might as well put it straight in."

"Down the side near the back door. I didn't know who else to call. I really appreciate you coming straight over. Thanks."

"No problem." Travis carried the broken seat to the bin.

Katy leaned over the railing and watched as he broke the chair into smaller pieces and binned them. His jeans hugged lean hips and long legs and his black T-shirt covered a chest and broad shoulders more impressive than she remembered. But what had she known when she was fourteen? Only that his smile had melted her teenage heart and Gran had kept a firm arm around her shoulders as she asked for his autograph. Back then he'd seemed carefree. 'Too cocky for his own good' Gran claimed as she steered Katy away from Lark Creek's favourite son. But she'd smiled fondly at Katy's defence of him and agreed he was a good-looking boy. 'Thank goodness you're too young to lose your heart to him, Katy. That boy's a heart-breaker if ever I saw one.'

"He still is, Gran," she whispered as Travis flipped the bin lid closed.

He wiped his hands on the backside of his jeans and strolled back to the veranda. "It was ready to fall to pieces. Just lucky your grandmother wasn't the one to sit in it."

A familiar prickling started in Katy's eyes. How long would it take before she could think of Gran without this awful sadness? She sniffed and cleared her throat.

***

Guilt slid down Travis' gullet and settled like a lump of lead in his stomach at the sight of Katy's sadness. Merle Leonard's passing without his knowing was yet more evidence he'd buried his head in the sand since his return to Lark Creek. Katy had been close to her grandmother and he'd just—insensitively—reminded her of her loss. "She was a lovely lady, your gran. Always kind to me and my family."

Katy surreptitiously wiped her cheek. "Thanks. So, what were you doing when I rang before? It sounded like I caught you in the middle of something important. Sorry about that."

"Doing? Ah—" *I was writing a song to your lips and how much I want to kiss you.* Like that would go over well. He turned his head a little more so his injured cheek was less noticeable. "Working in the study. There's a lot to keep on top of with a property the size of Thornyhill."

"I bet there is. Even Gran's house needs . . ." She looked up at the roof and frowned. "Repairs to the roof for a start. There's a lot of maintenance that needs to happen, and I'd love to do the house up."

"Is that what you're doing in Lark Creek? I mean—" How long had it been since he'd had a conversation with an attractive— make that a beautiful woman? Young Adam was more coherent than Travis and that was saying something. The boy was fourteen and as self-conscious as most teenagers. But Travis had made one stuff-up already. It was inconceivable he hadn't noticed Merle Leonard's absence when he'd skulked home, tail between his legs. And he didn't want to seem nosy, but he sure as hell wanted to know if Katy was going to be on the other side of his back fence for a while.

"Gran left her house to me and now I've got to decide what to do with it." She pressed her lips together and a little frown creased her brow.

Damn. It sounded like she didn't plan on sticking around long. *What to do with it* had the ring of doing the house up to sell. Adam appeared carrying a tray containing three tall glasses of juice and three plates almost hidden beneath thick wedges of a wickedly rich chocolate cake, which he set down on the cane table.

"Katy made the cake. Was that okay to bring it out?" He glanced at his aunt, and Travis noted a hint of vulnerability and uncertainty in the boy's manner. *Reassuring.*

"That was a good idea, Adam, thank you." Katy handed a plate and a glass to Travis. "If you're game to try another of Gran's cane seats, feel free."

Travis eyed the remaining chair and two-seater. They looked in slightly better condition, perhaps because they were protected against the wall of the house. But still . . . He moved to the stairs and sat on the top step. "I think I'll sit here and admire the view."

"Me too." Adam came to sit beside him and bit into his cake. The boy demolished half his slice with the hunger of the ever-starving teenager before he looked up at Travis. "How did you get your scar? Was it on your motorbike?"

Lulled into a pleasant frame of mind by the cake and the fact he'd been able to help Katy without facing anyone in town, Adam's questions caught Travis unaware. They fractured his peace of mind and turned the moist cake to ash in his mouth. They reminded him of all that had changed—and all that he'd lost.

"Adam, it's not polite to ask such questions." Katy's voice came as though down a tunnel. He heard her, but his mind filled with the noise of the truck's brakes, the screech of metal across bitumen, the sting as something cut his hand, his cheek, the coppery tang of blood in his mouth . . .

He should have been prepared for the curiosity, for the lack of social filters. But he wasn't. Casting a sideways glance at the boy, Travis sucked in a deep breath. He expected to see fascinated horror, but there was only youthful interest. Swallowing the cake in his mouth, he turned to fully face Adam.

"Yeah, an accident on a wet road. I was lucky not to be killed by the truck." There. He'd said it. He'd put it out in the world and the world would do as it damned well pleased with the information.

Behind him, Katy gasped. "You were nearly killed? How did you escape?"

"Luck, pure and simple. A split second or another inch and I'd have become a musical footnote."

"My God, Travis, I didn't know it was so bad. The news reported you'd been in an accident and that you were in a stable condition with non life-threatening injuries. To come so close to dying is—it's freaky."

Travis shrugged. "But I didn't. End of story."

"You're a musician? What do you play?" Adam pounced on a different part of his reply. Travis recognised the same light in his eyes as from his youth.

"Guitar mainly with piano and keyboard on the side. I write my own songs."

"You were listening to some of Travis' work last night, Adam. Remember the one about riding the highway?" Katy leaned her arms on the railing beside Travis.

"You wrote that? Cool! I tried to play it just using chords, but it doesn't sound the same as when you play it." Adam shuffled to his feet, juggling his plate and glass in the awkward, ungainly way of young lads grown too quickly and not accustomed to the space their bodies filled.

"Thanks. There are a couple of unusual chord progressions and a change of key part way through that you might not have picked up on. That makes a difference." He stood and set his glass and plate on the tray. "I'd better get back to work. Thanks for the cake. I don't think even my mother's chocolate cake was as good as yours."

Katy grinned. "Flattery will get you a slice to take home if you like."

"Tempting, but I don't fancy my chances bumping through the back paddock with a plate. How about you bring a piece with you when you and Adam come back? It will give me something to look forward to." His gaze dropped to her lips. Would they taste of chocolate cake?

"You're on. I'm hoping either tomorrow or the day after I'll be able to sit for long enough to drive to Dalton and then we'll pick up the paint and be on your doorstep an hour after that."

"Good, see you then. Bye, Adam."

Chapter Fourteen

Two days passed slowly. Katy checked her inbox every waking hour, but the hoped-for email from the producers of the renovation show failed to materialise. Not even an acknowledgement of receipt had arrived by the time she climbed gingerly into the driver's seat of her car and hope faded. But was it silly pinning all her hopes on the slim chance of gaining one of the coveted places on a reality home renovation show? Making plans—actual, realisable plans—with lists of steps to achieve them was the way forward. Her first attempt had been poor, but she had the same family genes as Rosie. And Rosie was the queen of list-makers. If her older sister could do it, Katy would learn how to.

Sitting on the cushion she felt unbalanced. Changing her posture to ease the pressure on her behind, she snuffed the engine the first time she tried to reverse out of the narrow garage. Adjusting the seat helped and she manoeuvred out far enough so Adam could get in.

"I could drive better than that." Adam seemed to be all arms and long legs and lean angles as he lowered himself onto the passenger seat.

"We'll see if that's true when the time comes. It's not the same as playing a video game."

They drove to the same home ware centre Adam had bought his spray cans from while Katy's CD of Travis' first album filled the car with his music. As she parked the car and switched off the engine and the music, Adam turned to her. "Katy, do you think it would be okay if I asked Mr Roberts to teach me guitar?"

Given the circumstances of their meeting, the question took her by surprise, not because Adam wanted lessons but because he was asking about Travis. "I don't suppose it would hurt to ask, but he's pretty busy running Thornyhill Farm. Don't be surprised if he doesn't have time."

"Cool. I'll ask him this afternoon."

"Only if we see him. I don't think we should bother him if he isn't out and about when we get there."

They picked up a can of undercoat and accepted the salesman's help in matching the topcoat colour, and stowed the tins in the boot. Before they left the store, Katy priced paint for the interior and exterior of Gran's house. Despairing of how to earn the money to begin the task, even if she did the work herself, she checked her emails. Still nothing from the television show.

When the CD began a repeat loop on the drive home she turned off the music and glanced at Adam. "I know you weren't thrilled about living in a one-bedroom apartment with your parents for three months, but how do you feel now about spending your summer holiday with me?"

"Aww, Katy, you're cool. It's just there's nothing to do here, and all my mates are back home."

"I get that. It was different for your mother and me when we were growing up because we wanted to get away from our mother's new home."

"Why?"

"She—didn't have a lot of time for us, but Gran always made us welcome. And we had each other, at least until your mother started work during uni breaks."

"She's a lot older than you, isn't she?"

"Ten years. But we did lots of things together. The creek was our favourite place. It's a shame the water level is so low or you could swim there."

"Yeah. But that's all you can do." Adam slouched in his seat.

"What do you think would make Lark Creek an exciting place for young people to visit?"

"Why would anyone *want* to come out here?"

"That's what I'm asking you. What would make things better—fun?"

"Adventure park, maybe. Paintball!"

Maybe the difference in their ages wasn't so great after all. Katy thought longingly of her zip line idea. "Active sports. Hmm, I wonder if there's a possibility in that idea?"

"Why? Are you planning on starting something?"

She indicated, slowed, and took the turn towards Lark Creek. "It's crazy, I know, but I've got this idea of turning Gran's home into a really nice B and B, but I figure Lark Creek, or at least the district, needs some sort of attraction to make people want to come here. I can barely afford to paint Gran's house, but maybe there are other people who have ideas and money to put into a venture that will bring tourists in. I've no idea how to find them though."

"Are we going home first to get the cake for Mr Roberts?"

"Oh, good call. I forgot we promised cake. Is there still some left?"

"Yeah. You told me to leave the last piece for him and I did. You make really great cakes. Do you think you could make another cake tonight?"

"You, my lad, are not subtle." She turned the car into the driveway of Rose Cottage. "But if you pop inside and grab that last piece of cake now, I'll think about baking later."

"You're on." Adam raced inside and came out thirty seconds later with a plastic-covered plate. "Got it."

##

Katy parked on the nearside of Travis' shed. They unpacked the paint from the boot and set it down in front of the graffiti-covered wall before she realised she had nothing with which to open the cans. She looked from the paint to the shed, and then at the house. Was Travis home? He hadn't come out to say hello and it was hard to tell with the curtains drawn and both front and back doors closed. She looked at the paint tins and the cake plate in Adam's hands. "I think we'll have to interrupt Travis. We can't leave the cake outside or the icing will run, and I forgot a screwdriver to lift the paint lid."

"I'll go." Adam had possession of the plate and he strode

away before she had a chance to remind him to be polite.

She put her hands on her lower back and stretched. The drive had left her with an aching bottom and a sore back, and she didn't relish the thought of sitting while Adam undercoated the wall. Stretching from side to side, a soft groan escaped. Maybe she could—

"Katy, are you still sore?" Travis came around the back of the shed, hoe in hand and a streak of dirt on his right cheek.

"Oh, hi. A bit sore, yes. Adam just ran up to the house with the last piece of cake, as promised." She straightened, conscious of looking as well as feeling dishevelled, and her hands slid down and pulled her top back over her Capri pants.

"Thanks." His gaze dropped to the paint tins sitting like guards on either side of her. "I see you've been to the paint shop."

"Do you have something to open the paint tins with? I forgot to bring a screwdriver with me."

"Sure. Come into the shade while I get you one." She followed him into the shed, stopping just inside while her eyes adjusted to the light. The shed was well organised with two large panels of pegboard on which every tool had its place outlined in black marker. Travis went straight to a toolbox and withdrew a screwdriver, which he handed to her.

"Wow. You'd never lose anything with this level of organisation. Why did you say to come inside while you looked for it? Seems to me you'd never mislay anything."

He shrugged and wiped his hands on a small towel before hanging it back on a hook at the end of the bench. "I thought you might find a few minutes out of the sun to be pleasant."

She nodded, unsure what to say. The Travis she'd encountered at their first meeting on the track the day she'd taken a tumble was a far cry from this Travis. It was as though he were two different men. Of course it didn't help that their first encounter had been when she trespassed on his land. But he'd taken her to the doctor and he'd come to Adam's rescue as soon as she asked for help.

"Have you done any more thinking about Merle's house, about what you want to do with it?"

"I've got some ideas, but no one to run them by."

He spread his hands, palms up. "I'd like to hear them."

"Really? I mean, I don't want to take up your time if you're busy, but I'd love to get someone else's take."

"Fire away."

She drew a deep breath and twined her fingers together. "It's a big house despite being called a cottage, five bedrooms and plenty of living space, on five acres. The creek runs close by and it has pretty gardens—at least, they will be once I've tidied them. I thought maybe I could turn it into a B and B. You know, make the property pay its way. What do you think?"

***

"I think it sounds like you're thinking of staying in Lark Creek." Travis liked the idea—a lot. As far as he was concerned the possibility of Katy not leaving town was a positive. "Have you started making plans? What sort of changes do you need to make to the house?"

"Painting for a start, and I think a few roof panels will need replacing. But I'm hoping—"

"Katy, I can't find Mr— Oh, you're here. Great, here's your cake, Mr Roberts." He handed the plate to Travis.

"Thanks. I'll save it for afternoon tea when I've washed off this dirt. Have you got everything you need to start painting?"

"Katy said we need a screwdriver to open the paint."

Katy held up the tool. "Got it already. Okay, Adam, come on. You need to get the undercoating done this afternoon so it has time to dry and then you can do the first topcoat tomorrow."

Adam took the screwdriver and headed outside. Travis stopped beside Katy. "I'd like to hear more of your plans sometime."

"For sure. I'd better go and keep an eye on Adam now though. I'm not sure how efficient he'll be with a paintbrush instead of a spray can." She gave him a quick smile and hurried out and around the corner. Moments later her voice rose sharply. "Not yet, Adam. You've got to stir it first."

Travis chuckled and shook his head.

Rather Katy than me.

He carried the cake plate into the kitchen and set it on a shelf in the fridge, and then washed off the morning's dirt. Before he headed into the study, he allowed himself one brief look through the window. Adam was assiduously applying undercoat to the wall while Katy stood in the shade of the peach tree his mother had planted in the vain hope she'd beat the birds to the fruit. Katy popped the top of a pen into her mouth and looked towards the house. He gave her a wave before dropping the curtain. A warm feeling expanded and filled his chest as he settled to work in his study. He'd promised himself the afternoon working on his new song and it felt damned good to be composing again.

He'd gone to ridiculous lengths not to show his face to anyone. Meeting Katy that morning on the track had felt like the worst thing that could happen. But she'd caught him unawares, seen his scar and not freaked out. She'd confronted his cranky, snarly side and given as good as he dished out. And since that morning, the music had begun to flow again. His first new song since before the accident was taking shape thanks to Katy.

And to Katy Leonard's lips.

As he concentrated on recalling her smile, her lips, and the sparkle in her eyes, the riff—*Katy's riff*—began playing in his mind. He opened the music software programme and set the notes out in black and white on the screen, before turning to his electronic keyboard. The beat was slow enough that even his injured hand could play a passable rendition. Satisfied he had the core of the song to his liking, he turned back to the screen and added another musical phrase to the score. The music began to take shape into something slower, more sensuous than his earlier work. The chord progression hinted at deepening emotions, but the theme eluded him. Was that because he was too focused on Katy's lips instead of the connection between singer and subject?

As he wrestled with the problem, his phone vibrated and he glanced at the screen. Kyle. For the second time in weeks, he answered his manager's call instead of letting it go to voice mail. "Yo, Kyle, how are you?"

"Great. And it's great to hear your voice. Really great, and on the chance you might say yes with enthusiasm—is it still okay if I visit you?" Kyle managed to sound upbeat over the brief hesitation.

"Sure."

"Really?"

Kyle's pleased tone came through the phone and reminded Travis it had been too long since he'd sat with a friend and just chewed the fat. Hiding away from everyone, he'd cut off all his connections. That stopped now. "Yeah, really. And bring a bottle of something decent with you."

"Is everything—okay?"

"More than okay. I'm writing again."

"Ma-aa-te! You don't know how much I've wanted to hear that. There's news, buddy, big news, and I want to see your face when I tell you. I'll see you tomorrow."

Travis ended the call and tossed his phone on the desk. Kyle wasn't the only one delighted he was writing again. All it had taken was one chance meeting with a raven-haired woman.

Who would have thought his muse was alive and well and living in Lark Creek on the other side of his back fence?

Chapter Fifteen

"Katy? I can't find my cargo pants. Have you seen them?" Adam's voice roused her from her online research.

"When clothes can stand up without their owner wearing them it's time they went to the laundry. They're in the wash."

"What am I going to wear?"

"Jeans? Shorts? Surely you've brought more than one pair of cargo pants with you?"

"Yeah, but I like the pockets on my cargo pants." He stomped off and moments later, the sound of his bedroom door slamming echoed down the hall.

Katy sighed and stared at the trees lining the creek. What on earth was she going to do to keep Adam occupied for the next few weeks? Rosie had said he could help with the renovations, but for that, she needed money she didn't have for paint and materials. After Adam finished painting Travis' shed, the days yawned before them. "I need a list of ideas and I need it now."

She minimised her browser and opened the word file she'd typed from her notes last night. Feeling rather pleased with her efforts, she began changing it into a timeline not dependent on having money to invest in the project. By the time Adam reappeared, dressed in shorts and an open shirt over a khaki tee, she had a plan. A real plan for the first time since Dad died. It was exciting and a bubble of goodwill towards Adam and her sister welled within Katy. If not for Rosie's request and Adam's presence, she might not have discovered she could plan a project. And if this worked out—*when* this worked out—what else might she accomplish? She smiled at Adam when he stepped onto the veranda.

"I'm ready. Can we go up the back way on Grandpa's motorbike?"

"I don't see why not. Dad kept an extra helmet in the shed. See if you can find it while I change my shoes. And check for spiders before you stick it on your head." Gosh, she was even beginning to sound like her sister in mother-mode. Was that what having kids did to a person?

As she shoved her feet into her boots and laced them, she thought about Adam's comments on the drive back from the home ware centre. Was there untapped potential for adventure tourism in Lark Creek? The idea should have been ridiculous, absurd even, but it tantalised her. The only people she really knew in town besides Geilis were Bessie and Travis. If he was around when they got to Thornyhill, she'd see what he thought of her idea.

Adam had the spare helmet on and the keys to the bike hung from his fingers when she walked down the back stairs. He held out her helmet, but clung to the keys. "How about you teach me to ride, Katy?"

"You're fourteen, not sixteen, and your mother would kill me." She slipped the helmet on her head and did up the strap, before adding additional painting gear to the back pannier.

A mutinous expression filled Adam's eyes. "My mates at school are allowed to ride."

"Probably their parents own properties where they can do what they like. And I'll bet when your friends say they're riding, it's on dirt bikes."

"It's not. Their parents let them ride motorbikes. Besides, we can ride up the paddock. If I'm not on the road you won't get into trouble." Trouble with a capital T peered down at her from Adam's blue eyes.

"Well, good on them, but I'm not your parent. I'm your guardian while your parents are away and I don't think teaching you to ride was part of what your mother asked me to do." She took the keys from him and swung a leg over the bike. "Are you coming? This was your idea after all."

Adam muttered a reply she couldn't hear through her helmet and climbed on behind her. She checked he was hanging on before she started the engine and flicked up the kickstand. The hard saddle seat was uncomfortable on her bruised tailbone and the ride along the creek and through Travis' bumpy paddock left her sore and a little out of charity with Adam. Her good mood and the pleasure she'd found in creating a plan dissipated in the face of his unreasonable expectations. The final straw was when he pulled off his helmet and tossed it on the ground.

"Stop behaving like a child, Adam."

"Why? You're treating me like a child. I'm fourteen, but you won't see I'm old enough to do stuff."

"Throwing a tantrum because I won't teach you to ride isn't the way to show you're not a child. Think about that while you paint today. Maybe if you show me I can trust you, I'll—I'll take you to the mini-cart racing track next week." God, now she was resorting to bribery. Learning to manage Adam's behaviour was more challenging than she'd imagined, and maybe Rosie would have handled his outburst differently, but at least Adam's mulish expression changed to something less confrontational.

He nodded and went into the shed to fetch the topcoat and brush. Katy hung her helmet on the handlebars and ran her fingers through her hair. How many weeks did she have to keep Adam happy and safe? Was a happy teenager even possible?

***

Travis twisted the fence strainer one more time and checked the tension of the bottom strand of barbed wire. He looked along the line of fencing he'd completed over the past week. A good if long day's work had finished this task and a sense of satisfaction filled him. He rose and a familiar clicking sound came from his knee. Since the accident, his knee complained like a retired footballer's instead of a fit thirty-one-year old. He leaned down and rubbed the joint. Flexing his right hand, which still hadn't regained full strength, he pulled out his phone with his left and checked the time. Kyle would be arriving soon. If he hurried he'd have time for a shower before his guest arrived.

Stowing his tools in the back of the ute, he realised he'd

probably miss Katy and Adam. Seeing her was one of the things he'd looked forward to this morning, but he couldn't let pleasure overtake the work that needed to be done on the farm. Not if he was going to take time out to spend with Kyle.

By the time he parked and put away his tools, the sun was setting, but he detoured via the shed wall to check Adam's progress. The first topcoat was in place, a bit patchy, but much of that would be disguised when the second coat was on. Certain Adam would think twice before graffiti-ing another wall, Travis checked the time again and hot-footed it into the shower.

He'd barely finished when a thunderous knocking sounded from his front door. Towel wrapped around his waist and water dripping from his hair, he hurried down the hall and opened the door.

"I see you dressed for the occasion." Kyle was dressed in his interpretation of *country*. His checked shirt and too-new blue jeans screamed R.M. Williams and his metro hairstyle was emphasised by the strip of short blonde-tipped Mohawk.

Travis shook Kyle's hand and gave him a quick man-hug. "Good to see you too, mate. Help yourself to a beer. Kitchen's through there." He dressed quickly and returned to find Kyle standing on the veranda looking out at the valley view.

"Not bad, hey?" He took the bottle of beer Kyle handed him and unscrewed the top. "Cheers."

Kyle tapped his bottle against Travis'. "Cheers. You know I'm a city boy through and through, but this place of yours has something. I can see why you wanted to spend time here."

"Spend time? You make it sound like I'm on holiday."

"You needed a break after your accident. Coming home to your roots is as good a way to recharge your batteries and recuperate as any."

"I told you I was going to pick up where Dad left off, not come out here to have a holiday." When would Kyle accept Lark Creek and Thornyhill Farm were now his home?

"What, are you a farmer now?"

"It's what I grew up expecting to be, Kyle."

"And then your music was discovered and you got the break most performers only dream about. You can't throw that all away on a whim."

Anger simmered just below the surface of civilised behaviour. "I wouldn't call these"—he pointed at his scarred cheek and his injured right hand—"a whim. I'd call them a damned good reason to step away."

"What? Do you think you're the first performer to have a scar? Give me a break."

"Would you pay to see me? Listening is one thing, but looking at this . . ." He turned and took a slug of beer. His lungs ached as though a giant band constricted his chest and the beer roiled in his gut. Writing music, even recording some of his work was still possible, but performing in front of a crowd? The very idea made him want to throw up.

Kyle's hand landed on his shoulder and squeezed. "Is that what you truly think?"

He swallowed the bile rising from his gut. "Yeah."

"Have the locals treated you like you're the beast from the Black Lagoon? I'd bet good money they haven't."

"I've hardly seen anyone. I order supplies online and get everything delivered."

Kyle frowned, turned and leaned his back against the railing, and studied Travis' face. "Haven't you been out at all?"

Travis shrugged. "A time or two. I prefer not to have to see people or have people see me." Katy's reaction had been less appalled than he'd expected, but she'd been injured at the time, and Dora and the doctor were used to dealing with injuries. He set them to one side. Other than them, the chemist's gaze had rested on his cheek a little longer than normal, but the man said nothing. Adam had seemed more interested in his music than his disfiguring scar. But they weren't *people*.

"Well I'll be damned. You've become a hermit." Kyle shook his head and set his bottle on the flat top of the railing.

Travis raised his bottle and drank before elaborating. "It's different among people I know and who know my family."

"How is it different?"

"It just is. Can we drop the topic now? I wouldn't have invited you if I'd known you were going to harangue me."

"You didn't invite me, I invited myself." Folding an arm across his chest, Kyle drained the last of his beer.

"Hmm. How long are you staying?"

"I figured overnight. You wouldn't turn a man away without a meal, would you? Especially one who brought two bottles of your favourite tequila with him."

"That sounds like bribery."

"Call it what you like, it's damned fine tequila. Hope you've got a couple of steaks to go with it."

Chapter Sixteen

By late afternoon as Adam cleaned his paintbrush and stowed the can of paint in the shed, Travis still hadn't returned and Katy had to accept she wouldn't get a chance to talk with him. Waiting for Adam had given her so much time to think. Now she was second-guessing herself and had begun to doubt her ideas for both the B & B and Lark Creek. No response from the television people to her application added to her usual self doubt, and by the time she parked the bike in the shed, she was ready to give up on the whole idea of the B & B.

"Can we have a barbeque dinner?" Naturally Adam's first words all afternoon were about food. Was it even possible to fill a teenage boy's stomach?

Happy to go with the easy option, she nodded. "Sure. I'll throw a couple of steaks on and—"

"I can cook steak and onions. Dad showed me what to do."

Gob smacked by Adam's offer, Katy tried not to let her surprise show. No matter how low her self confidence sat, she needed to build up Adam's by any means at her disposal. So she smiled. "That would be nice. I'll microwave a couple of potatoes and you can throw them on the grill to finish off too, if you like?"

"Okay." He headed off for a shower while she washed her hands and popped the potatoes into the microwave. It occurred to her that Adam's offer to cook dinner had to do with her comments about him behaving like a child. If so, she was happy with the outcome. She chopped two small onions and set the dish beside the steaks, wiped her hands and logged into her email. Still nothing from the television people.

For one long moment she considered calling Rosie in Japan and asking her advice, but renovating Gran's home—*no, not Gran's but my home now*—meant shouldering the responsibility for what she did and how she found the money to pay for it. "So it's onto Plan B."

When Adam reappeared, wearing crumpled clothes and with his hair wet, she forbore to comment. "Steaks are on the draining board and I've chopped the onions." The microwave buzzer sounded.

"Great. Thanks." Adam took out the potatoes, collected tongs and oil and set them on a tray beside the steak and onions. He looked organised and when he fired up the barbeque, he looked so much like his father Katy felt confident she could leave him for five minutes.

"If you don't need me for anything I'll just pop into the shower. Won't be long."

"How do you like your steak?" Adam called after her retreating back.

She turned, screen door in hand. "Medium-ish. Not running red, but not like leather."

"Okay." He turned back to the plate and dropped a piece of onion on it as Katy left him to get on with the job.

When she emerged from the bathroom, the aroma of barbequed onions and sizzling steak greeted her and her stomach rumbled in anticipation. Apparently Adam had learned from his father and was showing her he could be trusted with something as important as dinner.

"It's ready, Katy. Medium as ordered." He plated her dinner and his, and they carried the food to the gazebo.

Seated opposite him, she spread a paper serviette over her knees and picked up her cutlery. Adam sat like a statue across from her, holding his knife and fork in tight fists either side of his plate. "Why aren't you eating?"

"I'm waiting for you to start. Mum says the cook shouldn't dive into his food before the people he's cooked it for." Katy could imagine Rosie saying something like that. But Adam watched intently as she cut into her steak and tasted the first mouthful.

Surprised at finding it cooked as per her request, she grinned at Adam. "This is delicious. Thank you for cooking."

Adam expelled a breath as though he'd been waiting for that response. He shoved a piece of steak into his mouth and replied around a mouthful of food, "Dad taught me." He gave his full attention to his plate, hoeing into his meal and for several minutes they ate in silence.

When she'd taken the edge off her appetite, Katy set her cutlery on her plate. "Do you like doing other sorts of cooking?"

"Only barbeques. Dad says it's nice to give Mum a break from cooking sometimes."

"That's a nice thing to do. If you want to man the barbeque again we can build this sort of dinner into our weekly meal plans. Would you like it if I make another cake tonight? Same again?"

"Yeah, great."

As night fell, mosquitoes swarmed at the corner of the garden closest to the creek, their droning a counterpoint to the strident clicking of cicadas and the plaintive call of a night bird. Mozzies hid in low branches of trees lining the bottom of the yard, formed squadrons and attacked with a ferocity that finally drove Katy and Adam inside. "Back when I was a child, I had to spray repellent all over before Gran let me outside after dark. I reckon the mozzies from the creek are big enough to carry off a calf."

Adam gave her an odd look. "You know there's an old bathtub behind the shed, don't you? It's full of brown water. That's where they're coming from."

"The shed?" Katy tipped her head to the side and looked at Adam and her heart sank. *Behind the shed* carried possibilities of smoking out of her sight, or further forays into graffiti. *Behind the shed* sounded bad . . . and yet Adam had just told her he'd been there. Putting a gag on her instinctive reaction, she opted for a neutral response. "I didn't know that. What were you doing behind the shed?"

"Duh, looking for stuff to make a skate board. I thought there might be a piece of wood or old metal louvres like the ones above my window that I could use. I know I have to finish painting

Mr Roberts' shed, but then I want to do something fun. There's nothing to do here."

"I know." That was the crux of Katy's problem. Lark Creek offered nothing to attract visitors to the district. Unless she could change that, it wouldn't matter how much work she put into turning the house into a B & B. It would fail for lack of guests.

As they cleaned their plates, Katy's phone piped the ringtone for an unknown caller. She set aside the tea towel and picked up her phone, hoping against hope it was Rosie calling from Japan.

"Is that Katy Leonard?"

"Speaking."

"Aislinn Neilson from—"

"The renovation show." Katy's heart skipped a beat and she pressed a hand to her stomach as it clenched in anticipation—and dread. Was there any use in pursuing a renovation when there was nothing to bring people to town? Should she mention that or—

"That's right. I'd like to visit and assess your project on the ground, so to speak. Can you be available tomorrow afternoon?"

"Sure, yes, I'll be here. Thank you."

"See you then."

Stunned, she dropped onto a chair.

"Are you okay?" Adam eyed her warily, one hand in soapy water and the other holding aloft the meat knife.

"Yes. And no." Tension like a too-tight headband gripped her head. Gran's bequest of her home weighed her down like a ball and chain. There were so many decisions to be made, but she was on a rollercoaster racing out of control. If the visit tomorrow led to the offer of a spot on the show and Gran's home became a B & B, would she then be stuck with a white elephant no one wanted if it came time to sell? "I don't know what to do."

"Mum always makes a list of pros and cons." Adam pulled the plug and water gurgled down the plughole. Drops of water spattered her as he flicked his hands and wiped them on his jeans. "Night, Katy."

"Goodnight, Adam. Sleep well." She knew she wouldn't.

Chapter Seventeen

Travis pressed his hands to his aching head and slumped into a chair beside his manager. "That's the last time I let you talk me into tequila shots. Waste of good tequila."

"Mate, you're going soft living out here. We didn't even make it into the second bottle." Kyle lifted his chair away from the table and thumped it on the wooden floor with a grin that showed he wasn't suffering any ill-effects.

"You sound like a herd of elephants on steroids." A groan slipped through his compressed lips. "Besides, until last night I haven't had a single drink since the accident."

Kyle gave him a sharp look and leaned forward. "Why? You said drink wasn't involved."

"It wasn't. You know me better than that." Ordinarily Kyle's comment would have irked him. His Uncle Andy's alcoholism had ensured Travis treated hard drink with care, but his head pounded and his mouth was dry and he cursed tossing caution to the wind.

"Then—"

"Pain meds don't go with alcohol."

Narrow-eyed scrutiny drilled him, but Kyle had nothing to worry about. "I haven't been mixing them if that's what you're thinking."

"So you're off the pills now, right? You're feeling good, getting out working?"

There was a long pause that Travis didn't feel inclined to fill. Drumming pounded in his brain like he was front row at a rock concert, the thumping reminiscent of the consequences of his first teenage binge session. "I'll give you everything I own right now for a decent cup of caffeine."

"If I was a betting man, I'd accept. In your case—Trav, mate—you said you're writing again. Give me one good song and I'll do battle with your old-fashioned coffee maker. Or hair of the dog if you prefer. So—the song?"

"Coffee."

"The song is called 'Coffee'? Not sure that will grab your audience, but—"

Travis pushed to his feet and steadied himself against the table. "Need coffee for brain to function." He left Kyle muttering to himself and took himself off to the kitchen. The squeaking hinge on the cupboard was like nails down a blackboard and the hiss of gas scraped across his eardrums like a jet engine. He set a pot of coffee to brew on the stove before tossing a couple of paracetamol capsules down his throat and chugging a glass of water. As the reservoir filled in the coffee pot and caffeine-infused steam wafted through the air he leaned his forehead against an overhead cupboard and breathed in salvation. When the bubbling sounds stopped, he took down two mugs and filled them.

He drank half his coffee before he felt like moving again, topped up his mug and carried the two mugs back into the dining area. He set the second mug in front of Kyle and then leaned back in his chair. "Yeah, I've started writing. One song, not finished."

"Great. Tell me about it."

"No."

Kyle's mouth opened and closed and no words came out. He sipped his drink, set the mug on the table and tapped his finger beside Travis' mug. "How can I sell the idea of a new tour if I don't know even one of the songs you'll be singing?"

"Tour? You think I'm going to perform onstage again?" One word, four letters, unimaginable torture.

"Of course. That's who you are; that's what you do. You write, and you perform your music to an adoring audience who go out and buy your latest album and make us lots of money so you can afford to live and keep writing."

"Listen, just stop talking for once and listen, damn it. I'm writing, yes. It's one song so far—that's all. But I won't perform live again. Or on television, God forbid." The idea of thousands of eyes staring at him had never fazed him before the accident.

Before and after the accident. His life had been defined by a spill of oil on a wet road and now, just the thought of facing an audience of enthusiastic fans with his scarred cheek and faltering right hand sent fear prickling down his spine.

"Why not?"

Genuine confusion laced Kyle's words. Travis held up his right hand in front of Kyle's frowning face. Tequila tremors aside, his third, fourth and little fingers visibly shook. "Force 8 on the Richter Scale all on their own. Get it? Now, we're never going to have this discussion again."

Kyle stared at Travis' shaking hand before meeting his gaze. "It's better than it was before. Just give it time. If you're writing then you're also playing. I know you, mate. Music is your life and you were excited about the new song when we talked before."

"My hand is never going to be the same as it was *before*." How he hated that word. Hated what he'd become since that night. Lacking precision and control, unable to play what was in his head, unable to make music as he had *before*. His scarred cheek was visible and maybe easier to understand. But his unco-operative hand was the scar on his soul.

"Adapt your music. Play the melody and let someone else add the trills. There're plenty of good guitarists out there who'd kill to work with you."

Let someone else play his music? That was like telling them to take his balls.

"No." He pushed away from the table and stalked from the house. Of all people, he'd thought Kyle understood what playing his music meant to him. How it was part of him, so much more than notes on a page. And if Kyle didn't get that, maybe it was time to part company. Kyle called his name from the back veranda, but Travis kept walking. Down to the stables, past the opposite side of the shed where Adam had begun to topcoat the wall, into the stables.

Blinded by panic, anger, and a thumping head, he crashed

into a body. Sunscreen and a light flowery scent teased his nose as he held a pair of feminine arms and blinked, trying to see through a tequila sunburst.

Katy.

"Sorry. I hope you don't mind me being here."

Had he spoken her name? Conjured her from his subconscious because Kyle had asked for his song? Mercury whinnied a greeting and broke the odd moment. "I'm surprised. I thought you didn't like horses."

"I don't. Well, they're nice to look at, but I'd rather not ride one. I came into the stables hoping to find you, to talk to you and—"

"Can it wait, Katy? Now isn't a good time."

"Trav, there you are, mate. We need to sort this—" Kyle stood in the entrance, his attention swinging from Travis to Katy. "Well hello there. I see why Travis left me sitting alone. My name's Kyle, Trav's manager, and you are?"

Travis let go of Katy's arms as though her skin burned him and stepped away from her. He blinked again, seeing her as Kyle had seen her, a beautiful woman in short shorts and a crop top and sexy as all hell.

She extended a hand to Kyle. "I'm Katy Leonard, Travis' neighbour."

"Of course you are. Delighted to meet you. Any chance we might—"

Travis set a heavy hand on Kyle's shoulder. "You were about to leave."

"I don't have to. I can stay all day, another night, whatever it takes to convince you my suggestion is good. It will work."

Katy looked from Kyle back to Travis. "I didn't realise you had company. I'm sorry. Of course you don't have time now. I'll go and keep an eye on Adam." She took a couple of steps before turning back and twining her fingers together. "Oh, Adam won't be able to finish the topcoat before we go because we have an appointment this afternoon so we'll come back and finish tomorrow. I hope that's

97

okay with you?"

Yesterday he'd been sorry when he'd missed her. The promise of a return visit—and the interest in Kyle's eyes—encouraged him to settle things once and for all with his manager. "Fine. We can talk then. Or I could drop in late this afternoon?"

"That sounds good, thanks." With a half-wave, she left them alone.

Travis folded his arms and stared through the empty doorway where Katy had been standing. Now that Adam was almost finished painting the shed, he wouldn't see much of her. That thought left him feeling—oddly empty.

"Tell me about the song you're writing." Kyle set a boot on the bale of hay and rested his arm across his knee.

Travis flicked a glance at him and back through the doorway.

"It's about her, isn't it? I knew it the minute I saw her in your arms. You've found your inspiration." The grin on Kyle's face would have been comical if Travis hadn't been pissed off with him.

"I think it's time you were going." Sharing the music he was writing with Kyle, let alone with an audience of fans wasn't going to happen. It was personal, private, for him alone. "There is no new song."

Kyle shook his head. "I don't believe you. Writing music is like breathing for the rest of us. And that woman has given you CPR. I can't wait to hear what you've come up with."

"Not happening."

"A hundred bucks says you'll play it in front of an audience before Christmas."

"Fine. I'm so sure you're wrong I'll throw in a bottle of your favourite drink and you can do the same." The same old bet he and Kyle had made since they signed on together popped out of his mouth. His headache stabbed behind his eyes and he winced. *No more shots.* The damned bottle could sit and gather dust until Doomsday, but he would win this wager. "I'll see you Christmas Eve to collect."

Kyle rubbed his hands together. "My work here is done. And

to think I was worried you'd lost your mojo. So, I'll begin talks with promoters about a tour next year."

Anger like a hard ball of darkness filled his lungs and pitched in his stomach. "What didn't you understand before when I said 'no'?"

"I get it. No means—'not at this moment because I've a bitch of a tequila headache and I hate you when you're right'. Ah, but I'm banking on the delicious, de-lovely Katy to tempt you away from your farm and inspire a whole album of new songs."

"Don't put your life savings on that bet or you'll be camping in the stables with Mercury."

"I knew I could depend on you, Trav. Any chance of another coffee before I hit the road?"

By the time Kyle departed, Katy and Adam had packed up and left and Travis' headache was a dull throb behind his right eye. Wanting to see her and curious what she wanted to talk to him about, he waited until late afternoon to ride the motorbike down the paddock to Rose Cottage. Surely she'd be home from her appointment by then and happy for the chance to chat about her idea.

As he pulled up on the grass verge and tugged his helmet off, voices rose and fell from somewhere around the back of the house. The end of a white van poked out on the driveway side and he hesitated. Was that Fergus Campbell's work van? The thought had occurred to him that Katy might be getting ready to do some work on the house and needing a builder. Fergus would be his recommendation, but it looked as though she was one step ahead of him.

Since his return home, Travis had avoided everyone, including old friends. Fergus had been a good mate at school, easygoing, if shy. Reconnecting with him seemed less daunting now than before the day Travis had carried Katy into the doctor's surgery and faced Dora and the doctor.

There it was again—he was hung up on *before* and *after*.

Well, no more. He'd begun by reconnecting with Kyle. And if Fergus was out the back, well, he was an old friend. And Travis would deal with his reaction to his scars and move on. A flicker of optimism rose in his chest. Kyle's visit had been good for him and he'd make it the start of his new life in Lark Creek. He could shape his own *after*. He would make something new and good and different of the hand life had dealt him.

Head high, he followed the sound of voices and strode down the creek side of Katy's house. He turned the corner and froze. Katy was talking to a woman and pointing to something above his head. She stopped in mid-sentence and smiled at him, a smile just a shade too bright, too wide. "Hi, I'm glad to see you."

The interviewer turned towards him at the same time as the cameraman swung his camera around. Light blinded him, air whooshed out of his lungs, his chest constricted and tremors shivered through his body.

The woman's voice cut through his shock. "Oh my God, I'd heard Travis Roberts was in town. Benny, get this on tape."

Chapter Eighteen

Pleased to see Travis, Katy blurted out a greeting before her brain kicked into gear. Because she'd been thinking about him as the interviewer asked about her plans for the house. Because Travis knew Lark Creek and could answer questions about the local community that Katy struggled with. Because Katy was feeling desperate about speaking in front of a camera and Travis was a friendly face.

And then, "Oh my God, I'd heard Travis Roberts was in town. Benny, get this on tape."

Travis stopped, froze, and the smile he'd worn as he rounded the corner morphed into shock. A sharp, inverted vee deepened between his eyebrows and he turned his head to the left. His hands fisted at his sides.

Understanding hit like a bolt of lightning and her gut clenched. Travis was not only stranger shy, but also camera-phobic since his accident. From what he'd let slip she was pretty sure he hadn't even been into town until her accident had forced him to confront friends and locals.

She had to do something, anything to divert attention from him. Running on gut instinct, she laughed. "This is—Sam, a friend of mine. He fooled me when I first met him and he's fooled you too, hasn't he?"

Aislinn narrowed her gaze on Travis. "Yes, the likeness is— uncanny."

Benny lowered his camera and shifted the weight to his hip. "Do you still want me to film this guy?" Boredom leached through his question and Katy thanked her lucky stars for the cameraman's disinterest. Maybe she could still salvage the situation.

"Are you two an item?" Aislinn clutched at the possibility as though unwilling to let Travis go if she could make mileage out of Katy's visitor.

Travis was a good-looking man and he had a presence that lit up a stage back when he was performing. But it was clear to Katy that he had shunned attention since his accident. The quick angling away of his face said it all. She'd bet this was his worst nightmare. "Will you excuse me, Aislinn. I need to speak to Sam for a moment." With quick steps she walked towards Travis and took his right arm. His skin was cool, his cheeks, pale, and tremors shook his arm beneath her fingers. She managed to pull him around so his back was to the television people, managed two steps towards safety before Aislinn called out.

"How about—*Sam* comes back and tells us about Lark Creek, Katy? Some of the things you weren't sure about?" There was something in the way the woman hesitated briefly before the name Katy had christened Travis with—a hesitation that implied, at least to her guilty mind, that she wasn't believed.

"I'll be right back." Summoning a smile, she gave Aislinn a half-wave, tugged harder on Travis' arm and dragged him down the side of the house. They reached the far end before he stopped abruptly and dragged in a shuddering breath.

"Are you okay?"

Anger burned in his gaze, hotter than a record-breaking summer day. "Why the hell didn't you tell me you were doing a *television* interview?"

Katy took a step back from his scorching look and held up her hands like a shield. "Whoa there, *Sam*. I just saved your hide. Don't you dare blame me. You're the one who walked in on that interview—"

"Which I wouldn't have done if you'd told me about it this morning."

"I didn't *know* about it this morning."

"But you said you had an appointment."

"I meant I knew Aislinn was coming, but I didn't know she intended to begin filming."

"How could you not know something like that?"

Snark crept into her voice and heat into her cheeks, but she put her hands on her hips and challenged him. "Gee, I don't know. Maybe it was because she didn't tell me there'd be a camera at our first meeting?"

He pinned her with a flint-like glare and a muscle ticked in his cheek. "How much are you getting paid for this? What's the angle? A sneak peek at the face of a one-time star?"

Katy reeled back as though he'd slapped her. The accusation stung and stole her breath. Her stomach threatened to throw up the sandwich she'd bolted down for lunch before Aislinn's arrival. Shaking her head, she backed away from him, from the man she'd come to like and respect . . . damn it, from the singer she'd idolised since she first began choosing her own music. "That's not what's going on here. I'd never do something like that, but if you think I would, then you'd better go. Now, while I've bought you this breathing space. And don't bother coming down here again because I won't ever be at home if you do. And that gate at the bottom of your paddock—put a damned lock on it, weld it shut, do whatever you damned well please to lock yourself inside, but I won't be using it again."

Head high, she strode up the front steps and banged the front door behind her.

***

Travis glared at Katy's retreating back before casting a last look up the side of the house. Wouldn't it just make his day complete if their argument had been filmed by the cameraman? There was no one in sight as he stormed back to his bike. He slapped the helmet on his head, revved the engine loudly and took off like a hare past the creek and through the gate he'd left open on his outward journey. Damn Katy Leonard. How dare she give him his marching orders? How dare she say she'd rescued him? *Rescued!*

But like a fool he'd been seduced by her outer sweetness into thinking she liked him even with his scars. Of course she didn't like him. The television crew didn't just happen to be there when he visited.

I'd heard Travis Roberts was in town.

She'd probably faked that so-called tumble to trap him into talking to her and weasel her way into his life. Maybe she'd even sent Adam to graffiti his shed. Who knew what deceit she was capable of? And what about his self-deceit? Wilfully allowing himself to be blinded by Katy's beauty and sass, he'd let down his guard and allowed her to get close.

He roared past the fallen tree and took the 'L' shaped corner up to the house determined to seal off the bottom gate before night fell, but as he pulled up outside the work shed, his phone vibrated in his pocket. Jaw tight with anger he thumbed the green button. "What?"

A moment of silence—and then a voice from his past greeted him. "It's Rick—Peyton. Have I caught you at a bad time or—"

The question hung in the silence. Unfinished but clear nonetheless. *Or do you not want to talk to me?*

Travis drew a sharp breath. Dragging his attention from Katy's betrayal to the friend who'd been in his thoughts since young Adam's graffiti had brought Rick to mind, Travis jumped in. "Personal crap. Nothing important. How are you, Rick?"

"Good. I'm getting out of jail next week and I was hoping for a friendly face when I get back to town."

"You're coming home?" Travis took the keys out of the ignition, shoved them in his pocket, and headed for the house.

"My stepfather left me in no doubt I don't have a *home* with him, but yes, I'm coming back to Lark Creek."

"Great. Swing by my place and we can catch up." The invitation tumbled from his mouth before he thought about it. But did he really mean it? Sure Rick had been on his mind recently, and they'd been good mates once upon a time, but after the Katy-incident he was suspicious of everyone's motives. Who could he trust? Who wouldn't be trying to make a buck out of a connection with him? Who—

Travis rubbed finger and thumb over his eyes. Rick was

coming home and there probably wouldn't be many who'd welcome him. In hope Rick had reached out to his old friend and Travis was still thinking only of himself. A wave of shame and guilt engulfed him. His separateness from the local community was of his choosing, but Rick would find it just as tough to walk down the main street of Lark Creek. Everyone would stare at his mate just as Travis imagined they would stare at him and his scars.

A fine pair they made—the misfit and the misanthrope.

"Tell you what, why don't you stay with me until you work out what you want to do?"

Down the line came a soft inhalation of breath, and in the background, an authoritarian voice said, "Time's up, Peyton."

"Thanks, Trav. Appreciate it. See you next Wednesday."

The connection ended and Travis was left staring at the phone in his hand. Distracted by Rick's call, he went into the house and grabbed a beer from the fridge and carried it onto the front veranda. Leaning against an upright post, he drank a mouthful and watched the western sky blaze into gold and orange. On the far side of the valley a line of cows wandered in single file up the hill towards the Hamilton's farm and further around, lights winked on at Romney's vineyard and he tried to recall if it was harvest time. He frowned, before he remembered it was only mid-November. Harvest wouldn't begin until late January, which he'd have been aware of if he'd made any attempt to ease back into his community. Maybe it *was* time to do something.

He'd made Rick an offer and he'd see to it—somehow—that his friend got a chance to set his life back on track.

If only he could do the same for himself.

Chapter Nineteen

"Adam? Come on. Let's get this rotten painting over and done with and then we'll never have to speak to that louse again." Stomping down the hall did nothing to vent the anger simmering inside. She'd tried so hard to save the situation yesterday, but Travis' reaction had blown her away. A night tossing and turning at the injustice of it didn't help.

How dare he accuse her of taking money in exchange for photos of him? As if the *friendship* she'd thought was developing between them was fake.

But even after Travis left, Aislinn persisted in trying to get Katy to rope him into the project. She called him 'your boyfriend, Sam' with that same 'I-don't-believe-you' tone in her voice. And heaven knew why but Katy persisted in protecting his identity. Maybe she wanted to drive home the fact she wasn't like he thought. Not that he'd know or care.

Stupid, misplaced loyalty.

"Ready." The pockets of Adam's cargo pants bulged with who knew what. Right now, Katy didn't care. If there was a spare spray can she'd probably take great pleasure in writing what she thought of Mr Paranoia over the freshly painted shed herself.

Without waiting to see that Adam followed, she strode down the stairs and set off along the creek path towards the bottom gate. Adam loped along beside her, phone raised as he tried to make a connection.

He caught her eye and opened his mouth, but she held up a hand. "Yeah, I know. Lousy reception out here too. Everything's lousy, this sucks, but you'll be finished in an hour or so and then we'll drive over to the mini-kart track for the rest of the day. Does that sum it up right?"

He gave her an odd look as though she'd grown an extra head, nodded and shoved the phone into a pocket. "Thanks." They walked on in silence, each lost in their own thoughts until the gate came into view.

Clanging began in a series of triplets, the result of Travis wielding a mallet. He wore a welder's helmet with the face plate tipped up, but as she approached, he tossed the mallet down and picked up a piece of equipment which he set alight.

"Damn, he's going to weld the gate shut. Come on." Katy broke into a run and crashed into the metal gate just as Travis lowered the face plate and bent over the hinged end.

"Travis! Wait." She grabbed the rolled tube top and shook it hard.

Travis looked up, turned down the flame and raised the face plate. "What?"

"Can you leave that until Adam's finished painting your shed?"

"No."

"Well, can we come through before you start welding?"

"Read the sign." He turned the flame up, adjusted his helmet cover and set to work again.

Katy jumped back and turned away from the searing brightness. What sign? She'd been focused on Travis and the gate when she emerged from the creek track, but as she stepped back she could see a newly hand-painted notice on a piece of plywood. A dribble of red paint ran into the thin layer of what looked like white undercoat. 'No trespassing. Offenders will be prosecuted.' The day she'd meet him on the hilltop he'd accused her of trespassing and promised to close the bottom gate permanently. And then they'd embarked on a friendship of sorts and she'd forgotten all about it. Yesterday must have reminded him of his threat.

Frustrated by the loss of what she'd thought was Travis' friendship, and the unfairness of the charge he'd hurled at her, she turned and stormed towards the dirt track. "Come on, Adam. Mr Inconvenience-the-hell-out-of-Katy thinks he's being clever. We'll take the car and go round the long way. At least we can leave straight for the kart-track from Thornyhill when you finish."

But she couldn't leave it there. She couldn't let him have the last word. Not when he was so wrong about her. Ripping a page out of her notebook she penned a succinct statement telling Travis where he could shove his welder. Then she ripped the hair tie from her ponytail and wrapped the note around a river rock and lobbed it over the gate. It landed behind Travis' feet near the mallet. Dusting her hands off, Katy stormed back the way she'd come. If she was very lucky maybe he'd trip over the rock first. The thought gave her grim satisfaction.

Travis put the final weld in place, turned off the flame and tossed his helmet on the ground behind him. He wiggled the gate and spared a look at the creek track. Good. The little liar had gone. He turned to pick up the helmet and mallet and his boot clipped a medium-sized rock. A red hair tie held a ripped piece of paper in place. So she thought she'd have the last word, did she? Uncaring what she said, he couldn't stop himself ripping the band off and scanning the note.

It was brief and crude and to the point. And it made him angry all over again. Leaving tools scattered where they lay, he strode to his bike, shoved the helmet on and started the engine. He'd tell little Miss Liar what he thought of her.

To her face.

He made a tight turn towards the gate and pulled up in frustration. Katy could no longer ride up this way to his place, but neither could he take the quick route to tell her what he thought of her betrayal. Anger stoked by her note bubbled and boiled in his gut.

Revving the engine, he spun an incomplete donut and raced up the hill, past the fallen tree and slewed around the 'L' shaped corner fast and furious. The bike bounced over a ridge of hard dirt and skidded in a patch of gravel. His foot shot out, his knee cramped, the bike skidded one way and he rolled into the fence post.

Winded, he lay looking up at the sky one-eyed, his unstrapped helmet tipped over the other. Cautiously flexing fingers, ankles, knees, he worked his way around his body checking nothing was broken before he sat up.

The bike lay on its side a few metres away. He tugged off his helmet and tossed it in the general direction of the bike and leaned against the post.

Stupid, stupid, stupid.

Letting his anger with Katy's betrayal needle him into driving like a fool sent a fresh wave of anger washing over him, this time with himself.

"Mr Roberts, are you okay?" Pounding feet and jerky words drew his attention from wallowing in self-pity. He turned his head as Adam raced up the faint dirt track and slithered to his knees beside him.

Flushed cheeks in a pale face snapped Travis out of his pity party. The boy was scared for him. "I'm okay. Just catching my breath. What are you doing here?"

"I wanted to talk to you. Before you had a row with her Katy said I could ask you, but she left before I got a chance to. I heard the motor revs change and there was a screech of metal." Adam looked at the bike and back at him. Doubt tinged his voice and his hands lifted towards Travis, hung in empty air as though unsure of their destination or purpose, and then dropped into his lap. "Are you sure you're okay?"

"Yeah. My own stupid fault." Trying not to groan Travis levered himself up and wiped his hands on his jeans. Blood ran from a long, thin cut that crossed the scar on his right hand and his body was one giant aching bruise. Served him right for driving like such a bloody fool.

"Do you want a hand with the bike?"

Truth to tell Travis didn't want any company, but since the teenager had offered, Travis wouldn't knock back his help. "Sure. You grab the seat and I'll take the front end." When both had a grip on the bike, Travis counted them in. "Ready, and heave." The bike rose like a wounded beast. One side was pristine silver and red, the lines sleek and powerful. The other side was a nasty mess of dents and slashes through the red panel that reminded Travis of his face after the other accident. Bile rose in his throat and he swallowed to hold both it and the memory at bay.

The cut on his hand stung. He'd injured his hand that other time as well. He flicked away drops of blood and gripped the handlebars.

Adam eyed the cut and him, and opened and closed his mouth a couple of times before words formed and fell. "I can clean that for you if you like."

Travis drew a deep breath. As much as he wanted to be left alone, Adam's concern felt like a breakthrough with the boy, a small victory in atoning for whatever he hadn't done to help Rick when they were teenagers. "Thanks. Are you any good at making coffee?"

Adam bit his bottom lip and shrugged. "Instant coffee, yeah."

"Give me a hand putting this brute away and I'll show you how to make real coffee." Adam leaned into the task, but even with his help Travis' shoulder protested as he put his weight behind pushing the bike up the last stretch of hill. Great, he'd probably wrenched those muscles too.

They wheeled the bike into the shed and Adam dropped the kickstand and stood looking longingly at the bike. "She's a beauty. That's what I want when I get my licence."

Travis considered the bike from Adam's perspective. At fourteen, power and sleek lines had attracted him too. "Scarred as she is she won't be featuring in your aunt's film or whatever I walked into." Nor would he. Scars didn't make for good television. Scars belonged in horror movies and he had no intention of being used that way.

Adam shrugged. "Surface scratches. They don't make any difference to how she runs. Bet she goes like a dream." He froze in the act of stroking the powerful engine and met Travis' gaze with a look of uncertainty. "Katy didn't set you up with those television people. She got caught too."

Travis cursed his fuzzy brain as it snagged on that *caught*. Cursed it for caring enough to wonder how she could have been caught? Damn his headache and his spill on the bike. It almost paled yesterday's morning-after-tequila-shots with Kyle into insignificance. And damn the words spilling from his mouth. "What do you—"

"When she opened the door to those TV people that idiot shoved a camera in her face. That's what they do on that show. The first time they visit they try to catch out the people who are appearing. Dad said it's all faked, but Katy didn't know they were going to film her yesterday."

"She didn't know there would be a camera filming her for a television show? Come on, Adam, give me some credit for brains." Adam's defence of his aunt was understandable, nice even, though misguided.

"Of course she expected a camera later. But she thought the interviewer was coming just to check out the project. The woman told her she was visiting to *assess the project*. Katy didn't know it would be the first day of filming. And you know what, she wasn't expecting to see you until later."

Heat rose up Travis' neck and guilt prickled in his gut. "Do you honestly think she didn't know?"

Adam shrugged. "Mum says Katy would jump into a canoe on a river in Guatemala, wherever that is, and only ask where they were going later. When my oldies agreed to me staying with Katy for the holidays I was surprised. I didn't think Mum trusted her after all the things she's said about her."

"Like what?" He knew he shouldn't probe, but Adam's comments about Katy and her family intrigued him. And they gave him a respite before he considered that, just maybe, he'd been a self-absorbed, judgemental prick.

"How she hasn't held down a permanent job, but has moved every month or so since Grandpa died. And like how she hasn't saved any money and why would her gran leave her a house when

111

she hasn't done anything to help herself. Mum's pretty mean about her sometimes. I love the way Katy goes off on adventures and she's always been nice to me. You know, I reckon Mum is jealous of Katy."

Adam's words had the ring of truth. Katy had been nice to him too. Kind and caring.

"And me. I think I owe her an apology." How did a man go about telling a woman who had done nothing more than be nice to him that he was truly sorry for behaving like a total prick?

"Katy said . . ." Adam broke off and his cheeks flushed with embarrassment. "Never mind."

"Go on, what did Katy say?"

"I didn't mean to listen but you were standing right outside my window."

Understanding dawned. "About not being home if I called again. Hmm, that could be a problem. I might have to get creative to make her listen to me."

Katy said . . .

Unfinished conversation niggled in the back of Travis' mind as they walked back to the house. He left Adam rifling through the first aid kit for antiseptic and wipes while he washed dirt and blood off his hands. Katy hadn't managed to finish telling him her plans for Rose Cottage, nor what she wanted to talk to him about. Kyle had interrupted that conversation.

Words left unsaid . . .

Another verse of Katy's song began forming in his mind. What had she wanted to tell him?

Had Adam said why he'd followed Travis up the hill and he'd forgotten? He shook water from his hands and turned off the tap as Adam walked back into the bathroom. "What were you going to ask me? You didn't tell me, did you?"

"No. I didn't get a chance to." Adam tipped antiseptic onto a sterile pad and cleaned the cut on Travis' hand. It stung, and the pad came away streaked with red and minute specks of dirt. When he finished, he set the bloodied pad on the sink, reached for sterile gauze and covered the wound and bandaged it without meeting Travis' gaze. "Will you teach me to play guitar like you?"

Travis leaned against the sink. How the hell did he answer that? He couldn't play like he used to. And that was probably what Adam meant. Playing for time, he cradled his right elbow and indicated his injured hand. "Don't think I'll be able to make music for a while."

"But you could explain how to do stuff, couldn't you?" Hungry hope filled the boy's eyes and that need to help him, to do something positive silenced Travis' misgivings. If someone had taken time to guide his old school friend, maybe Rick wouldn't have ended up in jail. He was being given the chance to make a difference in a young man's life. He wouldn't refuse.

"What do you want to learn?"

"The fancy stuff you play on that highway song. Can you teach me to play that before I go home?"

"Do you have a guitar?"

"Yeah. It's nothing great, not like what you play."

"We'll have to clear it with your aunt." Only afterwards did it occur to Travis. Here was the opportunity he needed to speak to Katy. He would apologise and offer to teach Adam.

The question of whether he could make her listen in the first place consumed him as he handed over his practice guitar. Adam perched on the edge of a kitchen chair and ran his fingers down the strings before strumming a few chords. The boy knew his music. He plucked a little of the chorus of the highway song and looked up. Travis' promise to try had been enough to bring a smile to the boy's face.

***

Where was Adam? She'd been certain—maybe she'd just assumed—that he was following her when she stormed back to Rose Cottage. Her ears had been buzzing and a headache fuelled by lack of sleep and annoyance with *that man* had distracted her as she walked home along the creek track. Retracing her steps with her phone in hand and trying to find a connection so she could call him, she castigated herself for not keeping a better eye on her nephew.

She returned home and checked every room and the garden, and down behind the shed. She tried calling him on the phone from the house, but her call went straight to voicemail. By the time she trudged all the way back to Travis' welded gate, she was beside herself, her anxiety fuelled by ideas of alien abductors and axe-wielding psychopaths. "Adam? Where are you?" A lone crow cawed in response to her shouting. Desperate and worried by Adam's vanishing act, she climbed the gate. Thank goodness Travis hadn't seen fit to top it with razor wire—yet. Perching on a precarious toehold, she swung one leg, then the other over the top. She jumped, landed awkwardly and fell on her sore back.

Travis' tools were strewn over the sparsely grassed ground; mallet, here, helmet over there, blowtorch—the welding tool was expensive, but it looked as though it had been dropped with no consideration of its cost. Spidery tingles of fear rippled up from her stomach. Travis was neat, almost obsessively so with his tools. He would never abandon his gear like this unless something had happened to him or—*oh, God, please let it not be Adam.*

Panic clawed in her chest. Had something happened to Adam? Had he gone back to challenge Travis and— She couldn't think beyond that to what *something* might look like, to what might have happened. It didn't make sense, but her feet started running up the hill. Lungs pumped air and her arms pistoned as though she was in training for a sprint final as she forced herself to keep going up the steepest part of the path. At the corner of the paddock where an 'L' branch led to the house and sheds, she skidded to a stop in loose gravel. Pain shot from her damaged back muscles down her right leg, but it was nothing compared to her dread as she looked at evidence of what *something* might be.

Something looked like tyre skid marks and a fence post leaning at an angle. It answered none of her fears, only made them worse.

She moistened her lips, dragged a breath into impossibly tight lungs and raced towards the house, out of sight behind a line of small trees. As she came to the open door of the shed the fuel tank on Travis' motorbike reflected sunlight. At least a small, unscathed patch did. The rest was scratched and dented. She called out and glanced inside the shed. Travis wasn't there, but there were streaks of blood on the handlebars. Her stomach churned and her dislike of Travis took a back seat. That he'd had an accident and been hurt was clear. With no other option occurring to her, she ran to the house. Smears of blood marked the back door and she shoved it open without bothering to knock. "Travis? Are you here? Are you okay?"

She burst into the lounge room. Adam bent over a guitar and Travis perched his behind on the table next to him. Two pairs of male eyes looked up simultaneously and two mouths tipped up in smiles. "Katy, I'm glad to see—" Travis' smile faltered as she glared back.

"Adam Jefferson, put that guitar down and go home right now."

Chapter Twenty

"Are you okay?"

For a couple of heartbeats Travis thought his luck had turned as Katy flung herself through the doorway. Two heartbeats before he registered the high colour in her cheeks, heaving chest and untidy hair, and the fact wide wild-eyes were now glaring at him.

"Adam Jefferson, put that guitar down and go home right now."

Travis opened his mouth, but she held up a hand, gave him another glare before turning her attention to her nephew.

"Well? I've been searching the creek and the house for you. You disappeared without asking permission, there's bloody marks on the door and now I find you here with this—him."

Adam set the guitar gently on the table and faced his aunt. "Sorry, Katy, but I thought you heard it too."

"Heard—what?" Her gaze flicked between Adam and Travis, but he figured this was Adam's story to tell and his aunt to placate. When she'd calmed down, he'd apologise.

"The bike. Didn't you hear it? There was lots of revving and a horrible screeching sound and a bang. I jumped the gate and ran up the hill and found Mr Roberts. He came off his bike in gravel."

"I saw skid marks. And blood."

Travis held up his right hand. "Mine. Adam helped me get the bike back to the shed and cleaned up my hand. He did a great job, stayed calm in the face of an accident and patched me up like a pro."

"Right. Good." She huffed out a breath that sounded like frustration and relief battled and couldn't decide which won. "Come on, Adam. You need to finish painting *Mr Roberts'* shed, and then we can take ourselves off to the kart track and never darken his door again."

"But Katy, I—"

"Enough." The single word whipped out and stopped Adam in his tracks.

As Katy folded her arms Travis had the sinking feeling she wasn't ready to hear his apology. But he had to try. "Look, Katy, about what I said yesterday. I wanted to tell you—"

"You said more than enough. I don't care about anything you might have thought up since then."

Adam's fists clenched and his expression turned mutinous, and Travis decided enough was enough. The situation was becoming ridiculous. "Katy, stop lashing out at me for just one minute and let me explain." He turned to Adam and kept his voice calm. "Why don't you go and make a start on that last topcoat while I talk to your aunt?"

Adam looked at him and he gave the boy a slight nod and an encouraging smile. "It will be okay, I promise." The teenager shoved his hands into his pockets and slouched out the door.

As soon as the door clicked shut on her nephew, Katy turned back and glared at him. "Who do you think you are to tell *my* nephew what to do or to be making promises to him?" Her eyes sparked with anger. At least this time it was aimed in the right direction.

"Would you like a seat while I explain? It'll only take a minute or two."

"One minute. I'm counting down and then I'm leaving."

"Okay, I know you're mad at me—"

"Oh I'm not *mad* with you. *Mad* doesn't begin to cover how I feel about that awful crack about me using you to line my pockets."

Time was ticking away faster than he could get words of apology and regret out, and he sensed Katy edging towards the door. "I get it. I was wrong. And I apologise, completely and unreservedly."

That stopped her sidling to the door. But suspicion still glared at him from her flashing eyes. "You do?"

"I do. Katy, it wasn't your fault I walked into that television session, but—it threw me. I'm sorry if that sounds trivial to you, but until you showed up on my hill path, I hadn't even gone into town. I haven't seen anyone since I came back to the farm. Everything's been ordered and paid for online, and groceries have been delivered without me ever having to see the delivery man."

One eyebrow rose, her disbelief evident in the silent response.

"There's a heap of stuff I haven't dealt with—and then there's you. Your accident dragged me into town and made me see people again. I didn't like it, but I—I had to get over it to take you to the doctor. It was tough seeing and talking to even someone like Dora who I've known for most of my life. And it was a small step I managed that day, but when the television presenter recognised me through my beard and that camera swung onto me . . . I freaked and lashed out at the first person I saw. You copped the brunt of my panic attack and for that, I'm truly sorry."

Katy's lips pressed together, but at least she was no longer glaring at him. It was progress of a kind and he'd take whatever he could get. One eye on the clock, he realised his minute was well and truly up, but Katy wasn't moving. If he didn't count her tapping foot, or her lips parting and her tongue touching the corner of her mouth.

"So you now think that, despite the appearance of a television camera on the doorstep of Rose Cottage, I didn't plan some extravagant role play just to humiliate you? How can you be sure I'm not intending to sell photos of your face to the highest bidder to fund my renovation? I mean, clearly I need the money and just maybe you can't be certain what I'm prepared to do to get it."

Okay, she was still annoyed with him, but annoyance was preferable to hurt anger.

"You saved me by your quick thinking. I was stupid and illogical and paranoid when I jumped to that conclusion. Can you forgive me?"

Her gaze slid to the guitar resting beside him and she frowned. "Maybe. Why was Adam playing your guitar?"

He glanced down at his guitar. Letting Adam touch it, hold it, play it—no one ever touched his instruments. Ever. Like his music, it was his alone to play. He'd gritted his teeth as he handed the guitar over, but the teenager had treated the instrument almost with reverence. He rested his left hand on the body of the guitar and met Katy's gaze. "You said you were worried about Adam and what to do with him while he's visiting you. He asked if I'd teach him the tricky bit from the highway song and I said I'd be happy to, but only if it's okay with you. Is it okay with you, Katy?"

Her gaze flicked to his right hand and he realised he was cradling it against his chest. "You really did hurt yourself, didn't you?"

No sooner did she mention it than his injuries started throbbing. "I crunched my shoulder. Argued with a fence post and the post won. And this—" He held out his hand. "It's a cut and Adam really did do a decent job of cleaning and patching it. He's a good kid, Katy. He just needs to get over the disappointment of not spending the holidays with mates. Having something he enjoys—like playing guitar—will help."

She sighed and leaned against the doorjamb. "You're right and I've been trying to find things to do with him that don't cost an arm and a leg. He's grudgingly agreed to be my *gofer*-man, but thanks for making that offer. It's kind of you."

"I'm not kind, but I'm trying to say I'm sorry, and if I can make a difference in his life, then I will." Helping Adam was a way of paying another debt. Not that he planned on telling her about that one.

***

Katy's insides were still wriggling like a can of worms as she walked down to join Adam at the shed. He paused, paintbrush in hand, and cast her a look filled with anxiety.

"It's okay, Adam, we didn't kill one another," she said.

But now she understood something of Travis' pain. If she hadn't been so anxious about appearing in front of a camera, she'd have recognised his behaviour as the panic attack it was. Depression after life-changing events skewed one's perspective of the world. Like losing her father so soon after finishing her degree. How could she help others when she couldn't help herself? So she'd headed south, and north, wherever a whim or a casual position as carer drew her. Always on the move. Was she chasing something, or escaping? She had no idea, but she was curious about Travis' motives now he'd opened up a little. One thing in particular puzzled her more since his apology. Where she'd wandered, he'd hidden himself from prying eyes and she thought she knew part of his reason.

But not why he was desperate—*paranoid*, he'd said—to avoid the probing eye of the camera and the reporter. Sure, the scar on his cheek was noticeable even with his beard, but it looked as though it was fading and healing well. She had never thought he was vain, not like some stars, and yet he tried to hide his presence. It was almost as if—

No, it was absurd to imagine he was trying to fade from memory. A scar like his wouldn't stop him from performing. With talent like his why would he want to? She shook her head.

"What's wrong with it?" Adam's question drew her out of her musing.

"Pardon? Sorry, I was away with the fairies."

"I asked if you agreed to Travis' suggestion. He told you, didn't he, about teaching me guitar?" Paint dripped from Adam's brush into the hard-packed, dark earth as he stood tense and waiting. It hadn't registered in Katy's brain at the time, but Adam had been slowly picking his way through the key change of Travis' highway song when she burst through the back door.

"Yes. It's fine, though how he'll teach you with an injured hand I don't know. And what's with the name change? You usually call him Mr Roberts."

Adam grinned now she'd reassured him about lessons. "He said if he was going to teach me to call him Travis. Said it made him feel old to be called Mr Roberts and that was his father's name." He turned back to the wall and slapped on what was left of the paint on his brush. A trail of beige paint dribbled over the back of his hand

and Katy suspected there'd be blobs on his clothes that no amount of washing would remove.

She closed her eyes and tipped her face to the filtered light beneath the peach tree. Turbulent, emotion-filled encounters were draining and three within less than twenty-four hours left her wrung out and flat like a deflated party balloon. Her thoughts drifted to memories of her father and how safe and loved he'd made her feel; how devastated she'd been when he'd been killed on active duty. That had been the start of her roaming, her inability to stay put in any place or become attached to any of her clients.

Her eyes opened as the sound of boots crunched across gravel at the front of the shed. A moment later, Travis strolled around the corner. He sat on the hay bale beside her in the rapidly shrinking patch of shade and crossed long, jeans-clad legs at the ankles. "How's Adam doing?"

"See for yourself. Two rows of corrugations left and the job's done."

Travis nodded, but his gaze meshed with Katy's. Had they moved past suspicion and blame? Finding herself the focus of his non-hostile attention so soon after the intense confrontations they'd shared left her on shaky ground. She swallowed her uncertainty and searched for neutral topics, but he spoke even as she wondered what to say.

"You never finished telling me your plans for Rose Cottage. I'd like to hear them." His baritone voice rumbled pleasantly, sincerely, reminding her of her intention to ask for his suggestions about possible local attractions. Was it worth raising the question?

Lacing her fingers together, Katy drew her knees up and wrapped her arms around her legs. She'd start by telling him the easy part. "Gran left her house to me. I've no idea why. Rosie's the oldest sister. I would have expected it to go to her, or a half-and-half split at the very least."

"Rosie is Adam's mother?" Travis shifted a little closer on the hay bale and leaned back against the trunk of the peach tree. She was sure it meant nothing more than him making himself comfortable, but his knee nudged her raised foot and the heat of the day edged up a couple of degrees. Or was that just her? This morning she'd hated Travis with a passion. Now, his proximity and willingness to listen led her thoughts in the opposite direction.

She nodded and dragged her attention back to the conversation. It would be easier if she watched Adam painting the shed, but keeping her eyes off Travis was harder than it should be. Especially when his gaze dropped to her mouth. "Yep. Rosie's nearly eleven years older than me. Apparently Mum had a miscarriage sometime between us and my parents stopped trying to have another baby. According to Gran, I was an accident."

He frowned, no more than a brief tightening of his forehead, raised his right hand onto his left shoulder, and cradled his elbow against his chest. "I'm guessing she and Adam's father have a home already?"

"They live bay side in Brisbane."

"Maybe your gran wanted you to have a home of your own as well."

A home of her own.

"I never thought of it like that. You're probably right. It's the sort of thing Gran would think of, especially—" She shut down her runaway mouth. Why make it more clear to Travis what a rootless life she'd led since Dad's death? Gran had worried about her inability to settle anywhere, worried that, in her grief, she wasn't *living life but only existing through each day.* Katy turned her head as her nose clogged and tears blurred her vision. Gran's home was her gift of love to Katy, a way to give her permanence in a life filled with uncertainty and loss. Rosie had had Geoff and Adam to support her when Dad died, but Katy . . . She'd had only Gran. Had Gran known she was ill? Even the letter about scattering her ashes in the garden—was that about staying near her scatty, nomadic granddaughter?

"Katy? Why are you crying? Have I upset you?" A tentative touch on her arm reminded her where she was. And who she was with.

She sniffed, shook her head, turned to look at him—nodded. "I'm not upset. It's just—I can't believe I didn't see it before. God, and I even thought about selling her home! I don't deserve her gift."

"Whether you deserve it or not, maybe she knew you needed it." He handed her a neatly folded handkerchief with his initials, 'TJR' embroidered in the corner.

She ran her thumb over the embroidery and huffed what was intended to be a laugh before unfolding the hanky and wiping her eyes and nose. With a final sniff she looked at the initials embroidered on his hanky and then at him. "Let me guess, your mother's work, right?"

"You got it. Now she's living in Toowoomba she says she has time for all the crafts she didn't have time to do when she and Dad lived on the farm. So, what will you do with your gran's gift?"

So much love and most of the security she'd known in life had been under Gran's roof. Katy no longer doubted that keeping Gran's home was the right thing. It was the only thing she *could* do. She drew a deep breath designed to let her speak without crying fresh buckets of tears. "Okay, so the house has to pay its way somehow and the only thing I could think of to do was to turn it into a B and B. Bessie Jenkins, Gran's best friend since forever, she saw this renovation show on TV and told me I should apply, so I did. I got a call from that woman, Aislinn, the day before yesterday to ask if I'd be home so she could assess the project. Call me naïve or stupid, but I had no idea that meant they'd be filming me and the house straightaway."

"Interesting. I can see it working as a B and B, but—" He pressed his lips together and glanced at Adam and then shook his head. "I don't want to put a dampener on your idea."

"Tell me. Even if the television thing goes ahead—and Aislinn told me it would depend on what the head of programming thought of my project and yesterday's interview—I have reservations about its likely chance of success."

"Where will your guests come from?" His gaze softened as though he felt sorry for her and her stomach took a dive. She knew it, he knew it, and probably the television boss would recognise the problem too. Her idea was doomed by geography and lack of anything to bring people to their neck of the woods.

"Exactly. That's the flaw in my plan. I've wracked my brain trying to think of attractions that could put Lark Creek on the tourist map, but I'm stumped. Aside from one idea that is probably pointless—"

Adam strolled up with the paint tin in one hand and the brush in the other. Behind him the wet, newly painted section of shed wall glistened in the sunlight. "I reckon you need something adventurous. Like zip lines. You could put some down that hill above your place. That would be majorly cool."

Travis quirked an eyebrow at Adam. "And *majorly* expensive. But Adam's right. You need either a major attraction or several minor ones to link into. Otherwise there isn't any reason for people to come to the district."

"It's probably not worth doing up Gran's place if no one comes to town. But if I can't work out how to make the house bring in money, I'll have to sell it and—"

She gasped and wrapped her arms around herself as the thought of losing her last connection to both Gran and to Dad wrenched her very being. "I can't do it. I just can't. Travis—help me. What can I do to bring tourists to Lark Creek?"

Chapter Twenty-One

Travis sat at Katy's kitchen table and looked over the list they'd made. It was shorter than what he'd hoped for when he agreed to help. He set two sheets of paper in the middle of the table. One was covered in red lines and crosses; the other had two green-ticked entries and a green question mark. "The vineyard and the old pioneers museum twenty kilometres down the road are our best bets."

"Really? That's all we've come up with after an hour? Rosie makes lists all the time and she's successful. I thought there was some sort of magic in writing things down, but that list is kind of depressing." Katy sighed as she stood and collected their coffee mugs. "Another coffee?"

"Yeah, thanks."

She refilled the kettle and switched it on to boil. "It's disappointing when you think how little there is to keep people here let alone bring in the tourists. Cake? I experimented and made a caramel swirl this time."

"Sounds good. Hey, what about a cooking school? You could teach cake-baking."

"That's kind of sweet that you think my cooking is good enough. Now if my name was *Mary Berry*—"

Three sharp knocks at the front door were a welcome intrusion. Travis heard Adam's voice greeting their visitor and ushering them down the hall. Moments later Bessie appeared in the doorway. Her purple track pants and runners gave a clue to her mission before she spoke.

"Hello, Travis, good to see you out and about again. It's been too long. Katy dear, I was going to invite you to walk with me, but I doubt you'll want to given you have company."

"Hi, Bessie. You're always welcome. Coffee?" Katy gave her a kiss on the cheek and Travis pulled out a chair and held it with his good arm.

Bessie sat gracefully, her bright eyes darting from him to Katy and back to him. "Yes please. I was going to ask if you'd contacted those TV people yet?"

"I did, and they came for a preliminary look yesterday. Now I have to wait and see if the head of programming likes my project."

"I'm sure they will, dear, now that you have Travis on board." Bessie smiled and patted his arm.

On board? He wouldn't describe his meagre contribution in that way, but he was pleased to have a reason to work with Katy now that Adam had finished painting the shed. "Happy to help."

"Travis, can you show Bessie what we've been doing?" She turned back to the kettle and spooned coffee into a mug for Bessie.

"Okay." He sorted the pages on which they'd brainstormed into order with those marked in red as 'ridiculous or impossible' at the bottom and the most likely—the depressingly short two entries with green ticks—on top of the pile. The two maybes were little more than headings with a few dot points. Katy was disappointed. He knew it, even though she'd tried to hide her feelings and stay upbeat. Because without a reason to visit Lark Creek, Katy would have no guests and the B & B would fail. He didn't want her to fail. He wanted her to stay in town and he wanted . . .

What did he want from Katy?

Bessie tapped the table beside his hand. "Well, go on then and tell me. What were you doing?"

His gaze had gone straight to Katy as soon as he thought about her and Bessie had noticed. Heck, blind Freddie would be able to tell he was interested in Katy, and Bessie was sharp as a tack. Returning his attention to the list in his hand, he set it down in front of Katy's neighbour. "You know about Katy's hopes for turning Rose Cottage into a B and B, but there's a problem with that. What reason do people have to come to Lark Creek in the first place?"

"A good question. Do you have a good answer?"

"Not much of one. Close to town we have Romney's vineyard. It's good quality wine, but I don't know that's enough by itself to draw visitors out this way for more than a morning visit. And that's about it unless we go a distance down the road to the old pioneer museum." He pulled a map of the district closer and pointed at the location of the museum.

Bessie peered at the map and shook her head. "That closed a year or two ago. Is that all you've got?"

"'Fraid so. There just isn't anything to encourage people to stay overnight in town. Or to keep the young ones from leaving." The thought depressed him. When he'd left ten years ago, his career beckoned. It had been exciting, but he'd never thought of it as escaping Lark Creek. But lots of his old schoolmates had left town. Few came back because there wasn't anything to come back for.

"Why don't you call a meeting of townsfolk interested in revitalising our district? There may be ideas out there you haven't thought about."

Travis sat back as Katy set a mug of coffee in front of Bessie and took her seat. "You know, that's not a bad idea. If we can find somewhere to hold it and get the word out quickly, what about next Wednesday evening? Is that too soon?"

A public meeting was a great idea. It was exactly the sort of event guaranteed to gather ideas the two of them didn't know about. But Rick would be arriving that day and neither he nor his mate wanted the sort of scrutiny a town meeting would bring. "I'll have a house guest arriving and might not be able to attend, but anything else I can do to help, I will."

Katy's eyes widened and her lips parted as though she would speak. Bessie pressed her lips together, reached for Katy's arm and, when Katy turned, Bessie shook her head.

And Travis knew he was in trouble.

***

Travis wasn't coming to a meeting he'd supported? Why the hell not? But Bessie's hand on her arm stopped her and, as he pushed his chair back and stood, she realised he was cradling his right arm again. His mouth was pinched and sympathy replaced her annoyance.

She shouldn't be annoyed with him, not after his apology and his willingness to help, but her stomach clenched at the thought of running the meeting alone. Why would anyone listen to her ideas when she was still treated as an outsider by some of the townsfolk? It rankled in a way. Gran had been born here, as had her father, but because she'd been born in Townsville where Dad had been stationed, she was an outsider. But this was her future to make, and it was entwined with that of the town now she'd made her choice about Gran's home. "Okay. Any suggestions who to ask in particular?"

"The Romneys for a start. They have a tasting area they might be prepared to open for the meeting. I'll head home and make some phone calls and get back to you. You could make flyers for local businesses to stick in their windows once the details are sorted." He turned to go as Adam came into the kitchen. "Would you mind if Adam comes back with me and gives me a hand to open up the bottom gate?"

"Fine with me. Adam? Would you mind giving Travis a hand?"

"Sure. It'll be easier not to have to climb over it with my guitar." Katy smiled at the typical Adam-centric response. At least he was willing to help. She suspected there was an element of hero worship beginning to grow. "Dinner will be at seven so be sure you're home then. And Travis—you're welcome to join us if you like."

"Thanks."

Shortly after the sound of Travis' ute pulling onto the street filtered into the kitchen, Bessie set her mug on the table. "You've made a great start, but how are we going to bring that young man properly back into this community?"

How indeed? They'd had a fierce argument over the television interview, but this was his community, his people. Katy shook her head, uncertain if that was the sole reason for Travis' reluctance. But what did she know? "I wonder if it's just that he's hurting more than he's letting on?"

"Dear girl, I have no idea. But I do know he'll do a lot for you." Bessie stood and pushed her chair under the table. "Now I really must get out for my walk or I'll be coming home in the dark and that wouldn't do. My eyes aren't quite as good as they used to be at night."

"Sorry we took up so much of your time, Bessie."

"Don't you ever apologise for making me feel useful. I enjoyed it." She kissed Katy's cheek and headed for the door. "I'll call by tomorrow and you can give me an update and some of those flyers of yours before I go to my CWA meeting at morning tea. I'll pass on whatever details you've got and the ladies will spread the word."

Once Bessie had gone, Katy tidied away the mugs and plates and sat at her laptop to create a draft flyer. She printed a copy and set it on the table so she remembered to show Travis later.

***

"Travis, you just caught me. The surgery's about to close, but if you need something—" Dora had always had a soft spot for him, ever since his first visit the time he fell out of the tree as an adventurous five-year-old. She looked at his right hand which he'd raised to his chest without realising he'd done so.

"No, I'm okay, but I've a favour to ask."

"Fire away."

"I've been trying to get hold of Reg and—"

Her smile dimmed and she shook her head. "My brother's been taken to the hospital. He had a cardiac episode."

"Dora, I'm sorry to hear that. Is he—"

"He'll be okay, but it's given him a wake up call. They'll put two stents into one of his arteries tomorrow and he'll probably be home the day after, all being well. If it's important I've got a number for Geilis?"

"Little Geilis? Isn't she still in school?"

Dora chuckled and pushed her chair back. "You've been away a long while. Geilis has not long since finished a university degree in oenology. One day Romney Wines will be hers. That girl has got the devil of a business head on her as well as a clever palate."

"Where do the years go? Look, I'm not sure I should bother her if her father is in hospital. I only wanted to ask about using the tasting area for a meeting. It can wait." Everything could wait. His hand and shoulder were giving him curry and a headache had begun while he tried to help Katy brainstorm. Now he thought about it, he felt pretty lousy—the after-effects of another motorbike accident so soon after—the one he preferred not to think about. Tonight he just might have to give in and take a painkiller if he hoped to get any sleep.

"Why don't you let Geilis decide if it's a bother or not? Here's her number." Dora scribbled a number on the back of an appointment card and handed it to him. As he took it, the doctor walked into the waiting room.

"Mr Roberts, isn't it? Come on through. I'm sorry I didn't realise anyone was still here."

"It's okay, doc, I didn't come in for an appointment."

Her gaze ran over him in a cool, professional assessment. "Are you sure about that? What happened to your hand and your shoulder?"

Heat rushed up his neck as he confessed. "I fell off the motorbike and lost a round with a fence post. Young Adam cleaned up my hand."

"A fence, hey? Any cuts?" She took his right hand in her cool one and unwrapped the bandage. Even Travis had to admit his hand was a little swollen, and hot. Come to think of it, over the past hour or so he'd been feeling less than wonderful quite aside from a gnawing headache, but he'd put it down to a bruised shoulder and pulled muscles.

"Come on through. You probably need a tetanus booster shot and I'd like to check that cut more closely."

By the time Dr Manning finished, he wasn't sure which ached more—his right shoulder or his left bicep where the tetanus injection worked its magic. As the doctor put a fresh bandage over the newly-cleaned cut, she asked, "What caused the other scar on your hand?"

"That was when I went ten rounds with a truck." She raised an inquiring eyebrow.

"Wet road, patch of oil, just unlucky. Or maybe it's lucky. My bike was totalled. I walked away with minor injuries."

Dr Manning clipped the end of the bandage, but she didn't release his hand. She turned it over and made him work each finger.

"The bandage is fine, not too tight."

"I know the bandage is correct, but I'm wondering if you've been doing the right exercises to restore full functionality to your fingers. You're a musician, aren't you?"

"Yes." He couldn't manage more than that one syllable. *Full functionality*. His throat clogged and hope—so long locked away in a mental strongbox—jittered like a band of butterflies rising from a field of wildflowers in spring. *Full functionality—restored*. His throat rippled as he swallowed against the sheer hopeful surprise her comment raised in him.

She draped a sling over his shoulder and quickly and efficiently pinned his arm before slipping back behind her desk and adding his case notes to her computer.

"Is there—more I should be doing?" He was afraid to allow hope out of its box, but he wanted to, more than he wanted his next breath.

"It depends what you're already doing, but I'd recommend you visit a hand specialist I know in Toowoomba. Would you like me to set up an appointment for you? He's the best in his field, and he'll tell it like it is. If he can't do anything, he'll say so."

"Yes please." Travis waited while she called the specialist. She made a note and handed him the paper, and then covered the phone. "You can see Dr Terrison next Wednesday. He may be able to help you. Good luck, Mr Roberts."

"Thanks." On his way out to pay Dora, a strange sense of euphoria filled him. A sense of hope and change and—possibilities.

Dora processed his payment and handed him a receipt. "Before you go, I'm just wondering if you're interested in becoming a foster carer for rescue animals?"

"What, like foster parents for kids?"

"Something like that. You agree to look after certain types of animals for a period of time while the rescue centre looks for their forever home."

"Um, sure. What have you got—dogs and cats?"

"Yes, although they're easier to place. It's the bigger animals we struggle to find homes for, but you've got plenty of room on your farm. We have one very sad case at the moment and no one with the right sort of space to look after him. Can I send Samson out to you in a day or two?"

"What's Samson?" Travis had visions of a massive great bull with horns and attitude.

"A donkey. A very sad little donkey in need of love and understanding. Will you give Samson a home?"

"Sure. We'll give it a try." He'd ask Adam if he wanted to help look after the donkey while Travis' shoulder healed. Caring for a donkey in exchange for guitar lessons? That sounded fair. But first he had to tell Katy he definitely wouldn't make it to her meeting, not with Rick coming and now, this appointment in Toowoomba would probably mean he'd get back to town too late. After all the sharing and planning, how would that news go over?

Chapter Twenty-Two

Katy handed the flyer to Sam Carter, the butcher and began the speech she'd practised with Bessie. "Hi, I'm Katy, Merle Leonard's granddaughter. There's going to be a community meeting on Wednesday at Romney Wines tasting rooms and I was wondering if you'd mind helping spread the word to your customers and put one of our flyers up in your window?"

Sam glanced at the paper and set it on top of the glass-topped display cabinet. "What's the meeting for?"

"We're trying to find ways to bring tourists to the district and maybe increase employment prospects so young people don't drift away to the city." Her voice slid higher than she wished and she cleared her throat and continued, trying to sound confident. "Would that be something you'd be interested in participating in?"

"Wouldn't make much difference to my business." He looked at the skinny woman standing beside Katy. She was an old-for-her-years forty-something with a pinched mouth and hard eyes. "What do you think, Cass? Would your young fellow stick around if there was work here?"

Cass folded her arms across her chest. "He can't wait to get out of here, work or not. I don't see any meeting is going to change how he feels."

Katy's insides curled in on themselves and her mouth dried. This was exactly what she'd feared. No ideas, and no support or willingness to try something different. But *she* had to try. For Gran and her belief in Katy. "But that's the point. If there are jobs in the district, good jobs paying good wages, the need to go to the city to find work disappears, and people, especially young ones, might decide the lifestyle suits them and stay."

The butcher shook his head. "You're dreaming, love. But I'll put your flyer up anyway and tell anyone I think might be interested to go along. Now, what can I get for you today?"

Katy smiled although the effort hurt. "Three of those steaks and a kilo of mince please."

Similar responses met her request in each establishment. Genuine disheartenment looked back at her as she gave her spiel. Still, everyone took a flyer and promised to put it in their window. By the time she'd visited all the shops along the southern side she stopped and looked—really looked—at the main street of town.

When she'd visited Gran during school holidays as she'd been growing up, she hadn't noticed the gradual decline, an odd shop here or there that had closed its doors, the unmown lawns and overgrown gardens of an increasing number of vacant homes. Caught up in the freedom of playing along the creek until dusk and returning home only when Gran stood on the front veranda and called to her and Rosie to come in for dinner, she hadn't seen the lack of repairs, or the hopelessness in the eyes of older teenagers. Eventually, there weren't any young people hanging around the local café. Only when the Mykonos milk bar closed its doors did Katy notice, and wonder a little. Now, it was clear Lark Creek was dying. Was it even possible to resurrect it?

Tired and dispirited she approached a small café near the memorial. It was the only new business she'd seen in Lark Creek in years. As she pushed the front door open a cheerful high-pitched tinkling sounded above her head and savoury deliciousness wafted on the air. Her mouth watered and hunger tapped in her belly.

A young woman with a riot of tight red curls and a cheerful smile came through the door and stood behind the counter. "Hi, what can I get for you today? I've got fresh baked cherry tarts, vanilla slice, apple slice, sausage rolls and—"

Katy pressed a hand against her grumbling stomach. "I want to say one of everything, it smells so wonderful in here, but I'll go with a cherry tart and—could you do a flat white please?"

"Coming right up." The woman set a slice of tart on a paper doily-covered plate, and then turned to the coffee machine and flipped levers with the ease of long familiarity. "I've seen you up the street a couple of times. Are you visiting someone?"

"I've moved into Rose Cottage. It was my gran's home."

The young woman looked up and frowned. "Merle Leonard was your grandmother? I'm so sorry for your loss. She was a dear. She and Bessie Jenkins used to walk up here every fortnight for coffee and cake. I'm Darcy Carmichael." She wiped her hands on her apron and held one out.

Katy shook her hand and gathered her courage. "Katy Leonard. Look, I've organised a meeting to discuss ways to reinvigorate the town. I'm trying to drum up support. Here's a flyer. It would be great if you could come and bring your ideas with you."

Darcy set the coffee and tart on the counter and read the flyer. "Sounds great. I'm in. You know, the funny thing about this"— she tapped the paper—"is that it's taken an outsider to see the need and step up to the plate."

An outsider?

After all the holidays staying with Gran and now living in town, she knew she was still an outsider. Living permanently in Lark Creek wouldn't be enough for her to be accepted by some locals. It would take at least thirty years. Or a miracle, and miracles were in as short supply as water in the creek. She nodded, but her smile felt tight and her neck muscles ached with the stress of holding her head high and talking to so many reluctant locals.

Darcy tipped her head on the side and smiled. "I hope my comment about outsiders didn't offend you. I'm still waiting to be seen as part of the local community and I was born just down the road in Dalton."

"No, of course not. I was born in Townsville when Dad was stationed at the base up there, but Gran and Dad were both born in Lark Creek. It seems you can pass on your genes to your children, but not acceptance in your hometown."

"True. I should probably let your enjoy your coffee before it gets cold."

"Would you like to—I mean, unless you've got stuff to do

please don't go on my account. It's nice to talk to someone my own age." Until she'd started chatting, it hadn't occurred to Katy that she was lonely, but the prospect of enjoying a few minutes conversation with someone who wasn't negative about her idea was too good to pass up.

"Let me make a coffee and I'll join you. I'm not exactly run off my feet, as you can see." Darcy made herself a short black and took the chair opposite Katy. "I get the feeling you've had a bit of a tough time."

"Psychic, are you?" Katy sipped her coffee and sat back to enjoy the only truly positive encounter she'd had today.

Darcy shrugged and sipped her coffee. "You lost Merle not long ago and you looked—defeated when you walked in, as though you had the weight of the world on your shoulders. Tell me I'm wrong."

Was she that transparent or lacking in confidence? Maybe part of the reason she'd got negative responses was her fault. If she looked negative when she presented her ideas, why would anyone respond positively? "You're not. Honestly? I feel I've bitten off more than I can chew with this meeting. No one in my family thinks I can finish what I start, and I've lived up to their expectations all my life."

"I'll bet your grandmother didn't think that. She left you her house—at least, I assume that's why you're here."

"She did, but maybe it was because she knew I'd never manage to buy a home of my own."

"I knew your grandmother a bit. We chatted sometimes and she thought the world of you. One day she told me that your sister was the dependable, organised one, but you were the one with spirit who would achieve big things."

Stunned, Katy sat back in her chair and stared at Darcy. "Me? No, you've got that wrong. Rosie's the researcher. She's the one who'll make some fabulous breakthrough discovery. All I might achieve is turning Gran's home into a B and B."

The bell above the door dinged. Darcy looked up as a

customer stepped into her café and stood before she added, "That meeting sounds like a very sensible idea. I reckon your gran would approve."

Darcy moved behind the counter and served the workman while a warm glow filled Katy. Approval was rare and precious in her life. She was going to nurture Darcy's compliment and draw strength from it as she visited the rest of the shops on Main Street. And then she might drive out to the winery and talk with Geilis about the meeting.

At the thought of speaking in front of the townsfolk her stomach knotted again, but when she glanced up at Darcy, her new friend smiled. At least she had one ally in town, one person who thought her idea could work. Two if she counted Travis, three with Bessie. And Geilis. That made four people on her side.

Suddenly the day looked much brighter.

***

Travis pulled into the bus station in Toowoomba just as Rick's bus pulled into the parking bay. He slipped into a two-minute pickup zone and got out of the ute. Rick caught sight of him and gave a restrained wave before turning to collect a single duffel bag from the cargo hold. What effect would six months in prison have had on him?

Rick slung the bag over his shoulder and ambled across the concrete road, head down, but his gaze flicked from side to side. He'd always been a serious, quiet kid at school, but his expression was closed, giving away nothing of his feelings as he shook Travis' hand. "Thanks for picking me up. 'Preciate it."

"Mate, good to see you again. Lucky timing I had to come into the city today."

"Yeah." Rick slung the duffel bag into the tray of the ute and got into the passenger side. Travis drove out of the bus station and headed west. Rick turned his head and appeared to be taking in the scenery for a while. Once they were on the highway out of town, he turned back to Travis. "You're a sight for sore eyes."

"With this face? Hardly."

"What do you mean? Your scar isn't bad. Hell, when I heard you'd had an accident and got cut up, I imagined much worse."

"Did you imagine this?" He held up his right hand. Perhaps Kyle and the specialist were right. It was improving—slowly—and the specialist had been encouraging about the degree of fine motor skill Travis might eventually recover, but had cautioned it probably wouldn't be one hundred per cent.

I'll take whatever improvement you can help me get, doc.'

"What are you doing about it?"

"I've just come from the specialist. He thinks I can gain more control."

"And then you'll be back performing. Great."

"Is it?" Oddly, the idea of facing an audience seemed less confronting since his visit to the specialist. If he could play, really play properly—might he hold his head high again?

"You have real talent. Don't waste it."

Travis didn't reply, but Rick's assumption he would return to performing took root in his mind. Why wouldn't he play if he could? Music was his life. It was who he was. His music defined him and if he could play it, he should. Maybe one day soon, he would. And in the meantime?

He drove along the highway, heading into the westering sun before turning south. He had Katy's song to write and a new one that had begun to come together in his mind. And a meeting to attend if they made it back to Lark Creek in time.

Chapter Twenty-Three

The tasting room at Romney's vineyard was crowded and the low hum of conversation fed Katy's anxiety as she sipped more water. "Gosh, Geilis, I never expected this sort of turn out. How am I going to speak to so many people?"

"They're only here because of you, Katy. You're responsible for giving them an idea, a wisp of hope that there's something we can do to save our town."

"You should talk to them. You're the one with the pretty turn of phrase. *Wisp of hope*—that's good."

"Use it if you like, but you started this and you're going to move it along. Ready?"

"No, I'm not—"

But Geilis had stepped up to the counter and was already tapping a spoon against an empty wine bottle. "Listen up, you lot."

The hubbub subsided, a chair scraped, and all eyes turned to Geilis.

"You all know Katy Leonard, Merle's granddaughter and my friend. Well, Katy has called this meeting to tap into our hive mind. Please welcome her." Geilis stepped aside and led the clapping.

Katy stepped into her place, gripping the material of her skirt in one hand and her page of notes in the other. The paper shook like a leaf in winter wind. Her stomach flipped, clenched, threatened to heave out the water she'd drunk, but she swallowed and remembered Gran, remembered what was at stake.

This is it. No more Katy-Kate who never finishes what she starts. I can do this.

Looking for a friendly face in the sea of faces in front of her, her gaze found Darcy. The red-haired café owner gave her a smile and a thumbs up gesture.

"Go get 'em, Katy," Geilis murmured and sat on the last vacant seat.

Gran had taught her the value of a smile. And counting to ten before she spoke. Both had saved her when her mother's criticism—both silent and voiced—had stripped away Katy's confidence and stolen her voice, or made her want to scream in frustration at the unfairness of living away from her father. Katy cleared her throat and looked at her first dot point. *Greet everyone.* That was the easy part. She took a deep breath and fixed a smile on her face.

"Welcome, and thank you all for coming out this evening. You know from the flyers I distributed and which many of you were kind enough to display in your shop windows, that I had an idea—" Heavens, she was making a hash of even greeting everyone. She drew in another shaky breath and looked above the heads of her audience.

"That is, we need ideas to bring visitors to our town and our district. And to create jobs so young people—your sons and daughters—have reliable work to keep them here instead of heading off to the big cities.

"A few of us started thinking about what sort of things might provide jobs as well as attract visitors to Lark Creek. Currently— there isn't much."

"You're right about that, love." The male voice from somewhere at the back of the room was followed by a rising murmur of agreement.

"That's why we need what Geilis referred to as our hive mind. What she meant is that all of us together might be able to come up with ideas we can turn into a new direction for Lark Creek."

Darcy raised her hand and asked, "What have you got so far?"

"This place—Romney Wines is the only attraction we found within a twenty-kilometre radius. There used to be a pioneer museum in the next town, but Bessie Jenkins told us it closed down over a year ago. Shame, as that could have been a good drawcard. So, other ideas, suggestions? Let's hear them now."

Shuffling feet, creaking chairs—silence.

Katy's lungs constricted as hope fluttered like a zapped moth to the floor. It was worse than she'd feared. There was no hope, no one had any ideas, and her good intentions were doomed to die an insignificant death on the flagstones of Geilis' tasting room.

"Anyone?"

Just as she prayed for the ground to open up and swallow her, a middle-aged woman slowly rose and looked around at the assembly before folding her hands in front of her and looking at Katy. "I'm Janice Lehman. I teach in the primary school and I know that museum you mentioned. A friend of mine worked in it until it closed. They might be interested in reopening it with support from us, or maybe even moving it closer, somewhere like the old Lark Creek schoolhouse on Felix Road."

Sucking in a relieved breath that one person had accepted the challenge, Katy saw Geilis writing the suggestion on one of the winery's white boards and turned back to the schoolteacher. "Would you be prepared to explore that possibility, Janice?"

"Yes. I think there are a few people in this town who have skills they could contribute to improving on what Melville offered, but don't tell them I said that." She grinned and a few people laughed as Janice's offer broke the ice.

Geilis wrote Janice's name in a separate column and added, "Johnno can work a forge. He could demonstrate making horse shoes and decorative ironwork."

Excitement began to replace the worry that had dogged Katy all day, and she nodded. "Great. If we can get the pioneer museum up and running, either here or in Melville, maybe we can include a regular monthly event with food and displays. What do you think?"

A young woman with olive skin, her hair covered by a wide cream scarf, rose from a seat beside the French doors. "I am Samina. My husband and I, we have moved here from Afghanistan. I do not know if this is a help, but I can cook. For many people. Would that help this museum?"

Afghanistan?

Katy's stomach cramped and she missed the next few moments.

Geilis gave her a nudge and answered in her place, "What if we did a multi-cultural meal once a month? You know, damper around the campfire, and meals from countries where we've come from. Like Samina's Afghani food. Surely we've got a range of countries covered in our community?"

Katy stirred herself and concentrated on the idea Geilis had tossed out for consideration. "Do we have any Italian migrants here? If not, my grandmother taught me to cook Italian dishes pretty well."

A hand rose from somewhere in the middle of the audience, but the speaker remained seated. "We are Greek and my wife's *moussaka* and *Dolmathakia me kima* are out of this world."

Katy sought the speaker and recognised the face of the Mykonos café owner beneath a peaked cap. Iron-grey curls stuck out in wild abandon beneath the brim. Beside him, his wife smiled and leaned close to whisper something to her husband. "Thanks, Mr Alexopoulos, that sounds wonderful. I remember Mrs Alexopoulos's *moussaka* very well. The best I've ever tasted."

"That is true, and she misses cooking for lots of people, don't you, Rhoda?"

"Is true. You want me to cook *moussaka* for you?" Rhoda Alexopoulos stood and waved a hand across the crowd. "I cook for this many, no problem."

Katy's mouth watered at the memory of the delicately spiced Greek dish. "I'll be first in line if we can get this idea off the ground. Thanks."

"How about haggis?" A faint Scottish burr accompanied that suggestion from Andy MacAndrew.

Some wag called out, "Even in Scotland tourists don't like that one."

Laughter erupted around the older man, and he grinned. "Och, ye dinna ken what you're missing."

Brief though it was, the offers to cook and Andy's humorous

interjection pulled Katy firmly back into the present. A real sense of possibility was growing, and seeing all these people, Gran's friends and neighbours, coming together like this warmed her heart and filled her with hope. "These are great ideas, and with Janice co-ordinating the museum project, I think we are onto something good. But maybe we need more to draw people out here and make them want to stay longer. Overnight, or weekends in the country. What sort of things would make them come and then stay?"

Again there was no immediate response, but the quality of the sound was different. Murmurs filled the tasting room, murmurs that rang with a sense of 'what about this, how about . . .'

Movement near the door caught Katy's eye a moment before she heard a familiar voice.

"How about a music festival? Christmas in the Country." Travis' comment drew every eye to him and Katy's breath caught in her throat.

He came. He's out of hiding and facing his friends.

Her silly heart skipped a beat, then thudded with joy. Behind him, a shadowy figure leaned against the door frame, neither in the room nor part of the meeting. She couldn't see the man's face, but beside her, Geilis gasped softly and dropped the white board marker. She ducked her head and made a show of picking up the pen before turning her back on Travis and his friend.

Dora piped up from her front row seat. "Travis is just the man to anchor an event like that. Glad to see you made it after all."

"Sorry to be late to the party. I was out of town."

Geilis frowned as she wrote 'Country Christmas concert' on the white board. "Could we pull something like that off in the time we have left? It's barely six weeks till Christmas."

Most eyes turned back to Travis and waited as he stroked his short beard. "Maybe. I can make some calls if you think it's worth a shot?"

"We'd need everybody behind it." Katy turned to the townsfolk and asked, "Who wants to try?"

A chorus of voices rose in assent and Katy leaned against the counter. "Looks like we have our idea for this year. Now we need people to organise different parts of the show."

Travis crossed his arms, a look that was a cross between disbelief and eagerness on his face. "I'll look after the programme. I've got a few friends who might like to join us and a manager who hasn't had enough to keep him busy lately."

Geilis turned her back on Travis and the man behind him. "I think I can speak on behalf of Romney Wines and my dad and say we'd be proud to supply the wine."

"Thank you." Katy gripped her friend's hand and squeezed, lowering her voice so only Geilis could hear. "It's happening, isn't it?"

Geilis nodded as Janice Lehman stepped forward. "I know a bit about organisation and persuading people to help." There was laughter and a few groans.

"Don't we know it!"

Janice's cheeks coloured a little, but she continued as the banter died down. "That's enough from you, Rory Donovan and yes, I'll be expecting you to lend your muscles and maybe your trailer to the endeavour." The young man groaned and clapped a hand over his eyes in mock protest as Janice turned from pointing at the farmer and met Katy's bemused gaze. "I'd be happy to head up a committee."

"Done. Thank you. I think we should have a brief break for coffee and wine and informal discussions and come back with any other thoughts in—say, fifteen or twenty minutes. And maybe the gentleman at the door can make sure nobody escapes before you've signed up for something."

As people began standing and stretching and moving to queue for a drink, Travis strolled over and joined Katy.

***

"Travis, thank you for coming. I thought—well, I'm glad you made it." Katy's eyes glinted and her cheeks were pink as she put a hand on his arm.

He found it hard to believe he was here himself and the rush of adrenaline that had carried him over the threshold still raced through his veins. "You thought I wasn't coming, I know. I surprised myself, but when we got back into town and it was still early we decided we might make your meeting after all."

"Your idea is brilliant. I'm gobsmacked. And I'm so happy."

It made him happy to see what his gesture meant to Katy. It seemed such a small thing to do for her, and yet it had taken all his courage to step into the brightly lit room and speak in front of so many familiar faces. But if Katy could face the crushing fear she had of speaking in public, how could he do less? "I've had enough of hiding from everyone in town. It's more than time I started involving myself in what's going on."

"Right now, at this moment, I could kiss you for coming."

His gaze dropped to her mouth and a different heat—one that had nothing to do with the warm night and everything to do with his intense focus on her lips—rushed through his body. She tucked a strand of hair behind her ear and stepped away. Was she afraid she'd do just that—kiss him?

"Can I get you a drink?"

"Thanks. Maybe a glass of Geilis' wine?"

Katy turned to where Geilis had been standing but her friend had dashed into the back room as soon as Katy had called for the break. Katy slipped behind the counter and reached for two glasses and a bottle of white wine. "Geilis hid this before the meeting began. *'So we can celebrate straightaway when you realise what a success tonight will be.'* Katy mimicked Geilis' tone and then laughed as she poured a generous serve into each glass and offered one to him.

"Thanks." He touched his glass to hers and sipped. "This is good. Is this one that Geilis had a hand in?"

"It's her first solo effort and yes, it's delicious. You said 'we'. Who's the man with you?" Sipping her wine, her gaze roamed over the assembled crowd and the small stretch of bluestone-paved outdoor area.

145

Travis turned, but he knew Rick wouldn't hang around once the break had been called. "Didn't you recognise him?"

"He didn't come into the room, and besides, I was so nervous I wouldn't have noticed a green alien with tentacles waving. Who is it?"

"Rick Peyton."

Her glass seemed to hang in the air midway to her mouth. "What? But I thought he went to jail?"

"He did. He's done his time and now he's out. I've offered him a place to stay until he finds his feet."

Chapter Twenty-Four

"Oh." Quickly raising her glass to cover the reaction unleased by Travis' news, she took too big a mouthful of wine and began coughing. At least choking on Geilis' wine gave her an excuse not to answer. But what should she do?

She remembered the dark-haired man with the deep blue eyes. It was difficult to imagine that somewhere between clearing her grandmother's gutters and Gran's seventy-second birthday, Rick had gone off the rails. She couldn't recall the details of his conviction, but Gran had been shocked. And disbelieving. 'If Rick Peyton is guilty, I'll eat my hat,' she'd said more than once. Katy needed to find out more about Travis' house guest. Maybe Geilis knew more.

But Rosie . . . Rosie would kill her if she let Adam anywhere near Rick. No way would Rosie allow Adam to go to Thornyhill for guitar lessons if Rick Peyton was going to be there.

Katy cleared her throat and checked her watch. "I think we should get back to it. Where's Geilis?"

"Maybe we should just start and she'll catch up taking notes when she comes back." Travis picked up the whiteboard marker and twirled it between the fingers of his left hand. "Or I could scribe for you if you like?"

"Good idea. Thanks." Maintaining a business attitude would do until she worked out how to delicately and politely break the news to Travis that she wouldn't be a responsible guardian if she allowed her nephew to visit someone Rosie would deem *undesirable*. The idea sank like a lead weight in her stomach. It wasn't fair and it wasn't right, but she knew her sister.

The rest of the meeting passed with a couple more tentative ideas put forward, but the main focus was discussion about Travis' country Christmas music festival idea. As they helped Geilis carry trays of glasses and mugs into the kitchen, a few people led by Janice stacked the extra chairs and tidied the tasting room.

Travis backed through the swing door and held it open with his hip for Katy to pass. As she looked around for a space to deposit her tray her gaze snagged on the tall, dark-haired man stacking the dishwasher. As though he felt her gaze on him, he stood and held himself straight, neither speaking to her nor looking away.

"Rick—hello."

"Katy. I'm sorry to hear about Merle. Your grandmother was a kind and fair woman."

Fair? What did he mean by that? "Thank you."

Geilis came through the door with her father. Reg Romney had aged since last time Katy saw him and sagging shadows underscored his tired eyes. But his face lit up with a wide smile when he saw Katy. "Hello, sweetheart. Lovely to see you again." He kissed her cheek and gave her an awkward, one-armed hug. His left arm rested at his side and belatedly, Katy recalled his *incident*.

"How are you feeling since your visit to hospital, Reg?"

"A lot better than before, I can tell you." He turned to Geilis. "Have you moved those boxes into the cellar, love? Remember the temperature is important—"

"At all stages of the process. I know, Dad. I'll do it now."

Reg caught Katy's eye. "If I have to grunt to lift it, it's too heavy. That's my new mantra since they put the stents in. I'm not planning on being stupid about this second chance I've been given."

"I can help, if you like?" Rick's offer was hesitant, and Geilis visibly bristled, but Reg seemed pleased.

"Thanks, Rick. Appreciate that. There are a lot of boxes and they've been sitting outside since the delivery truck called late this afternoon."

"Do you want me to come with you and help?" Nothing Katy could put a finger on, but tension fairly crackled in the kitchen.

Geilis flicked a glance at her father and then pinned Rick with a firm look, the one that said he'd better not mess with her or there'd be hell to pay. "It's fine, thanks, Katy. Might as well make *good* use of the muscle on offer."

The only response Rick gave to Geilis' veiled insult was a muscle that jumped in his cheek. He nodded to Reg. "Happy to help, sir."

Katy dragged her gaze from their retreating backs and looked at the pile of mugs still to be washed. "We'll finish stacking the glasses, Reg. And I wanted to say thanks for letting us use your tasting room for the meeting."

"My pleasure, sweetheart. Just doing our bit for the community. It's a good thing you're doing. Merle would be proud of you. Now if you'll excuse me, this ancient man is going to toddle off to a hot milk and bed. Good night, Katy. Night, Travis."

Blinking back tears that sprang to her eyes, Katy murmured her goodnight. Would Gran be proud of her? Comforted by the thought, she reached for a new tray of mugs to add to the glasses.

Travis began filling the dishwasher from the other side. "He's right, Katy. Your grandmother was always proud of you, and she'd have been first in line to help with this idea of yours."

She nodded as memories surfaced, of Gran smiling in approval—when Katy mastered a new dish or reported back on the success of a technique in dealing with her mother. Unlike her mother, Gran had always encouraged Katy, and given praise when it was due. And when Katy had graduated with Honours in her social work degree, Gran had made the long bus trip to Brisbane for her graduation ceremony. Katy's mother had allowed a charity function to take precedence over her daughter's graduation.

"Thanks."

"I've got another idea—if you're agreeable to it." Travis' voice was low, and the brief hesitation sparked an image of what his other idea could be.

What I'd like it to be.

She pushed in the full drawer and closed the dishwasher door. "So long as it doesn't involve me having to speak in public again, I'm all ears."

Travis' chuckle sent warmth trickling through her veins.

"Aren't you going to emcee the concert? I'm disappointed."

Warmth turned to ice, elephants stampeded through her stomach and she stared at him, open-mouthed and afraid. "You *are* kidding, aren't you?"

His mouth tipped up in that one-sided smile of his. "Got you."

As relief crashed through her she folded her arms across her chest. "Not nice, Travis Roberts. I thought I'd die when I had to speak to that lot tonight."

"And yet, you did. And you got through that television trial interview, and very well too from what I saw."

"Like you were there for much of it. My knees were shaking and my mouth was dry. It was only that they surprised me at my own front door that carried me through it."

Travis' gaze pinned her to the spot. "You're stronger than you think, Katy. You can do whatever you set your mind to and I reckon Merle knew that."

Was Travis right? She hadn't felt in control of anything since Dad had died, and Gran's passing had left her bereft. Who was there now to believe in her if she didn't believe in herself?

Travis believes in me.

"I'll drop in tomorrow evening if that suits you and report on progress after I've made a few calls. What do you think if we aim for the Saturday night of the weekend before Christmas?"

"Perfect. I'll start work on flyers for the locals and work on a press release, unless that's treading on the preserve of your manager?" Katy wiped down the draining board and dried her hands.

"Why don't you draw up the draft information, then Kyle can put the spin on it and distribute it. He's got all the social and media contacts—television, papers, radio; he's a magician with all that stuff."

"Great. So, see you tomorrow."

Geilis and Rick entered through the door to the cellar. A cobweb hung from Geilis' hair and Rick had a streak of dirt on the shoulder of his white T-shirt.

Katy looked at them and turned to Travis. "Hey, why don't you all come for dinner?" *Rosie can't object if Travis' house guest comes with him to dinner. And Gran was a good judge of character. If she welcomed Rick into her home, so can I.*

Geilis swiped at the cobweb and screwed up her nose as it stuck to her fingers. "Dinner at your place sounds good. What is it— a war council or just a social gathering?"

"Work. Travis is going to let us know which of his artist friends is on board with the idea."

"Thanks, dinner would be nice, wouldn't it, Rick?" Travis looked at his friend, his one-sided smile and slight nod encouraging Rick to agree.

"As long as it's okay with Katy," Rick said with a glance at Katy.

Geilis dived in, her eyes narrowing on Rick. "You do know that Katy's looking after her nephew, don't you? If you know anything of Rosemary, her sister, you'll know she'd freak over having an ex-con in the same block let alone the same house as her son."

Rick's gaze hardened into a brilliant ice-blue. He shook his head, skirted Geilis and the stainless steel counter and stopped with one hand on the door. "Maybe you're right. Katy, thanks for the invite but I'll fix my own dinner."

"No, Rick, you're more than welcome. In fact, I'll be offended if you don't come."

"Maybe some other time." Rick pushed through the swing door, which quickly cut off the sound of his boots crossing the flagstone floor.

"Damn. I hoped— Never mind. Thanks, Katy. I'll see you tomorrow night." Travis flicked a curious look at Geilis before he followed Rick through the door.

Katy flopped onto a wooden stool and leaned back against the cupboard. "What an evening! I feel terrible. You were right about Rosie. I know she'd have my head if I allowed Adam near Rick, but the funny thing is, Gran always maintained he wasn't guilty and I respect her ability to judge character."

Geilis' smile vanished at the mention of Rick's name. She picked up the tray of empty bottles and took two steps towards the cellar, stopped and met Katy's eye. "She could have been right."

"Really?"

Geilis shrugged and a hint of colour rose in her cheeks. "Who knows, but there's something behind that mask he wears."

"What—"

"Don't you have to get home to Adam soon?" Abruptly she turned and shouldered open the door into the cellar and disappeared, leaving Katy to make her way home alone.

Chapter Twenty-Five

Travis handed Rick the beer he'd requested and settled into the canvas chair in the dark on the veranda of his home. Overhead, the sky was clear and stars hung like diamonds scattered across the Milky Way. In the distance, a curlew cried, its call mournful on the still air.

"Geilis was right about that sister of Katy's." Rick leaned on the top rail and tipped the bottle to his mouth.

"But it's not fair on you."

"I'll live. Isn't Katy's nephew the one you said put graffiti on your shed?"

Travis nodded. "Yeah. I felt I had to make the point to Adam that actions carry consequences. Katy brought him over every day until he finished repainting my shed." All in all, the arrangement and the outcome had been positive for Adam. *And me, if I'm honest. I found my muse the day Katy came into my life and Adam kept bringing her back day after day.*

"Sounds like you succeeded in teaching him that lesson."

"It helped. I'm not sure he was the only one who learned a lesson though. If it hadn't been for Katy, I'd still be hiding myself away from everyone."

They sat in companionable silence drinking beer until a mosquito buzzed below Travis' ear. He slapped at his neck and hoped he'd got the little blood-sucker. "Another beer?" Travis held out his hand for Rick's bottle.

Rick handed over the empty and stretched. "No more, thanks. If you don't mind I'm going to sit out here for a while and look at the wide open sky."

"Do as you like." He pulled the screen door open, but stopped at Rick's next words.

"Listen, Trav, thanks for picking me up and giving me a place to stay. I appreciate it. Just don't let the fact that lots of folks around here won't be so welcoming stop you from joining in things."

"Mate, until tonight I've been out in public exactly twice since I came back to the farm."

"Why?"

"Long story short? I was kidding myself it was because of my scar."

Rick snorted. "Yeah, if I had a face like yours I'd hide it too."

"Thanks." Travis had missed this, missed Rick's keeping-it-real attitude and easy company. "I see it wasn't enough to scare you off."

"Like I said this arvo, I expected it to be much worse when I heard about your accident. And, mate—I saw your motorbike on the news. It was a miracle you came out of that alive."

"Yeah, real lucky." Travis took a deep breath. "It's my hand that's the real problem. I haven't been able to play my guitar like before, but the specialist I saw today has given me a bit more hope."

"And that gave you an extra kick of courage tonight? Good."

"It was about time I got off my arse and stopped feeling sorry for myself. See you in the morning."

"Night."

Travis lay awake long after the sounds of Rick settling into the guest room faded. Restless energy filled him and finally he gave up sleep as a bad joke and sat in front of his computer. But staring at musical notes on a screen wasn't much better. He picked up his acoustic guitar, the first one he'd bought with his own money, and carried it onto the veranda. Quietly strumming it, he sank into its mellow sound and watched the stars glide across the heavens.

As he played, his fingers instinctively found the riff—Katy's song. Without conscious effort, the key changed, and the tempo. Every encounter with Katy changed the music and he had no idea why. It was frustrating and wonderful—and frustrating again. Mercurial, like Katy.

He strummed the riff, and then finger-picked it. Which one was his muse? Or was she both? And what did her lips taste like?

A discordant and totally out of place chord lifted the hairs on his neck and jangled down his spine. His fingers stilled on the strings.

What did *Katy's lips taste like?*

How could he write the song without experiencing a kiss from his muse? It wouldn't be like any other kiss he'd given or shared. Because Katy wasn't any other woman. No other female of his acquaintance—not his mother nor Katy's bossy older sister—would have succeeded in making him come out of his home. No one else had made him *want* to come out of hiding.

He needed to kiss Katy. But if he were honest, it wasn't about finding the truth in the song. He wanted to kiss her. He wanted it more than his next breath.

He set his guitar aside and was halfway across the yard before he realised it was still night and he was no Romeo to be visiting his Juliet in the wee hours of morning. He was no Romeo full stop. Why would Katy even consider kissing him?

'Right now, at this moment, I could kiss you . . .'

Pleased to see him, pleased to have his public support, she'd dropped the cliché into the conversation. It was just a saying.

And yet her blush and the way her gaze dropped to his mouth—not his scarred and damaged cheek, but his mouth—raised a tiny bud of hope.

He'd make the calls to fellow performers and he'd report in person to Katy. Tomorrow night he'd drop down to Rose Cottage for dinner. And he'd ask Katy for a kiss.

Chapter Twenty-Six

As Katy finished vacuuming the lounge room carpet, her phone vibrated in her pocket. She switched off the vacuum cleaner and checked the caller ID. Her breath caught in her throat and her lungs constricted as though she wore the corset she'd modelled for a friend's fashion retrospective. "Good morning, Aislinn."

This was the make or break moment for her and for Rose Cottage. Either the television manager had liked her interview and her project would go ahead, or she'd made a complete mess of it and her idea was sunk. But either way, Lark Creek was going to benefit. Somewhere along the way her efforts to retain her inheritance had been subsumed by the greater need to revitalise the town.

"Katy, I showed your tape to the programme manager. He doesn't think there's enough of a change to warrant investing the station's money . . ."

Hope crashed like a kite when the wind died suddenly, deflating, spiralling into a snarl of branches. Rose Cottage wasn't going to get so much as a facelift let alone a complete makeover. Not until Katy found a job and started saving enough money to pay for materials herself. Because, in spite of being rejected by Aislinn and the producer, Katy was sure a B & B could make money once Lark Creek was on the tourist trail. "I'm sorry to hear that, but I'm not surprised. I realise it was a long shot and—"

"Unless—"

The word hung in the air, weighty with possibility, loaded with second chances. "Unless . . . what?"

"Come clean with me, Katy. Your *Sam* is Travis Roberts, isn't he? Frankly, my producer was beside himself when he saw Travis walk into the shot. With him on board, even though your project doesn't really fit the guidelines for our show, the presence of a star like him could make your renovation the hit of the season."

"I—he—" She couldn't deny it without lying, and Katy

couldn't tell a lie to save herself. But neither could she let the station know they were right, that Travis was living in Lark Creek when he'd made his dislike of the limelight patently clear. What had he called his response to the camera—*a panic attack*? How could she do that to him? It was one thing for him to offer to organise performers for the Christmas event, but he hadn't said he'd be playing. He hadn't made any move to return to performing, and she couldn't be the one to dump him in view of the public. Grabbing at the only thing she could think of to throw Aislinn off the scent, she cleared her throat and crossed her fingers. A white lie was still a lie, but it was the best she could come up with. It was the only response she had half a chance of making Aislinn believe. "Sam wouldn't—Sam isn't—he doesn't like cameras."

A muffled voice, perhaps someone in the background of Aislinn's office, murmured indecipherable words before Aislinn responded. "We're prepared to add an extra ten thousand to the pot—undisclosed on the programme, of course—to sweeten the deal. What do you say, Katy? You get your B and B and we get a ratings boost."

***

Travis woke gritty-eyed and restless and fully dressed in yesterday's clothes. Hot and sticky, he remembered thinking about kissing Katy. After all, if he hadn't kissed her, how could he miss her kisses, and yet, miss them, he did. But had he actually walked down to Rose Cottage and asked Katy to kiss him?

Rick knocked on Travis' open door and stood in the doorway. "Prince Charming is awake—good. There's someone here to see you."

Travis groaned and sat up. His mouth was dry and his right hand ached worse than usual. "What? Who is it?" He swung his legs over the side of the bed and rubbed both hands over his face. His beard felt rough and his brain, foggy, with a lingering sense of foreboding. Surely he hadn't been stupid enough to walk to Katy's last night and ask her, had he?

"It isn't Katy, is it?"

Rick grinned. "Unless she's gone grey overnight, no, it's not her."

"Give me two minutes to get dressed and—"

"Don't bother. You'll only need to change again after you've seen—" Rick chuckled. "Just get your lazy self up and outside now. It's wrong to keep a lady waiting."

Travis shoved his feet into his boots, the only item he'd apparently seen fit to take off last night, and headed for the front door. A four-wheel-drive with a horse float attached was pulled up at the bottom of the drive. Beside the float, Rick stood talking to Dora Romney. When she caught sight of Travis, she waved, but continued talking.

"Ah, Travis, good morning. Sorry to wake you, but I wanted to catch you before you headed off to some far flung fence line.

"Hi, Dora. What can I do for you?" He glanced at the float. Rick's grin grew wider and there was a glint in his eye that boded no good for Travis' peace of mind.

"I've brought Samson out to stay with you. It's so kind of you to offer to take him."

Travis could feel the frown taking over his forehead, feel the tension ratchet higher in his brain. "Who or what is Samson?"

"You offered to look after a rescue donkey." Dora took his elbow and guided him to the open back of the float. "Meet Samson."

A skinny-boned donkey was tethered to the bar, its withers facing Travis as he peered into the shaded interior.

"He looks like a bag of bones."

"He's not had a good life so far. But that can change, starting with you caring for him until he gets a bit of meat back on his bones and we find him his forever home."

"Right. The rescue animal thing. Got it." With a resigned sigh—after all, he had promised Dora he'd help—Travis climbed in and reached for the halter. He manoeuvred the donkey around and guided him to the opening. Samson stopped abruptly, tugging on

Travis' arm as he resisted exiting the float.

Travis turned to look at the recalcitrant animal. Bright sunlight revealed a bare patch on the side of his neck and a slashing scar running diagonally across his long nose. Rick's grin faded. Dora put her hands on her hips and pinned Travis with a look that mixed compassion and determination, but her voice was gentle.

"You'll be good for him, Travis. He just needs time and a little TLC."

The combined efforts of Travis, Rick and Dora were needed to encourage Samson down the ramp of the float and across the yard. When the little donkey saw the open door of the stables, resistance turned into a stumbling run. Once he was inside, he headed into the first open stall and stood with his head in the corner.

"What happened to him, Dora?"

"We don't know much except that he came from a farm a few miles south of Dalton. Police closed down a meth lab operating there after a tipoff to the local council. None of the animals was in a good way. One of the horses and two dogs had to be euthanized, but Samson clearly had a spark of life left in him. It took three police officers to get him out of his stall there and into the horse float. They brought him to our shelter."

"What do you think I can do for him?"

"He's afraid to go outside—why, we don't know, but I suspect it's somehow tied up to the abuse he suffered. Show him kindness and try to give him back pleasure in being out of doors." Dora backed away and wiped her hands down her jeans. "I've got to go change and get to work. Good luck."

Travis leaned on the railing and watched Samson lip the wooden wall support. "I have a strange feeling Dora just sucked me in."

Rick carried a bucket of feed and tipped it into the trough. "So? What's the problem? It's not like you're going to turn Samson out."

"Of course not." But Dora knew a thing or two about

damaged souls. It wasn't much of a leap to see she equated Travis'
problems with the donkey.

Chapter Twenty-Seven

"I hope it's okay to drop in without—oh, hello, Geilis, Adam." Travis cut short his apology as Katy came down the back steps with her second guest in tow.

Adam was manning the barbecue and Geilis was chatting to him. In truth, Katy had been pleased when she opened her front door and Travis was standing there with a folder of notes and a bottle of red wine.

"Hi, Trav. You came alone?" Geilis peered around Katy's shoulder.

Twin furrows of disapproval appeared on Travis' forehead, but he refrained from commenting. "Of course. I've teed up several friends who've agreed to perform. My manager, Kyle, is setting up some interviews—"

Silently applauding his restraint, Katy wondered about the tension between Geilis and Rick Peyton before Travis' comment registered. "Interviews—for you?" Katy knew she sounded surprised, but she was certain Travis would avoid anything on television.

"Two radio interviews so far, but Kyle wants your copy as soon as possible. Once that's distributed, he'd like to meet you and—" Travis' sentence tailed off into silence and closed lips that sent a premonition of disaster sliding down her spine.

"Why does he want to meet me?"

"I'll just—" Geilis backed away and became busier than need be setting the table under the pergola. She turned on the string of pink and blue Chinese lanterns and lit the hurricane lamp and set it carefully at one end of the table.

Adam turned off the gas and scooped meat, onions, and corncobs still in their husks onto a serving platter.

"I'll tell you after we've eaten, when I can show you what we've got planned so far." Travis wouldn't be drawn further. "This looks great, Adam. I'm impressed."

They demolished the steaks and Katy's layered garden salad and Adam was clearing the table when Geilis' phone rang. She excused herself and moved away from the table with a quick apology. "Sorry, Mum said she'd phone if she needed me." Adam picked up the tray and carried it inside, and she turned to Travis.

"You said you'd tell me once we'd eaten."

"I did, didn't I? But first I have a favour to ask before Adam comes back."

Apprehension slithered like a spider down her spine. Finding herself alone with Travis shouldn't be a big deal. Until tonight, it would have been the stuff of her teenage dreams, but the unsettled feeling had everything to do with that look when he arrived. As though something had changed—or was about to. So many changes—each one associated with loss. Right now, she couldn't handle any more *changes* in her life.

"What sort of favour?" God, even her voice squeaked like a frightened mouse. What did she think was going to happen? Geilis was in muted conversation with her mother not ten metres away and Adam was likely to bound down the stairs like an overgrown puppy at any moment. She cleared her throat and tried again. "What do you want, Travis?"

His gaze dropped to her lips before he drew an audible breath and glanced at Geilis. Not six inches from her fascinated gaze his Adam's apple bobbed up and down, and he sat back on the bench, putting space between them. "I'd like to invite Adam to play at the concert, if you think his parents would approve. It would be a chance for me to teach him and occupy some of his time in a useful way."

"Oh." Why was she disappointed? Because she'd thought Travis wanted to kiss her? Wasn't Travis offering to teach Adam a coup and an answer to one of her problems? And yet . . . she *was* disappointed. Without realising how much she wanted her teenage dream of kissing Travis to come true, she'd half hoped he might be interested in her grown up self.

"Well, what do you think? Is it okay if I go ahead and invite him to play with the band?"

She gave herself a mental shake and offered him a genuine smile. "I expect he'll be thrilled and I don't imagine Rosie and Geoff will object. I think they'll probably be ecstatic he's gainfully employed." She sketched air quotes around the last two words, knowing how Rosie would jump at the offer. "I'd better go inside and—"

Geilis appeared at her side, her face pale against the night sky. "I've got to go. Dad's been trying to move stuff in the storeroom and a box fell on him. Mum thinks he's broken his arm."

"Do you want me to come with you?" Katy jumped to her feet, sending the bench seat clattering to the ground.

Travis rose and reached for his phone. "Is he trapped? I'll come and—"

Geilis held up both hands and shook her head. "It's fine, but thanks, both of you. Apparently Dad got Mum to call—Rick—before she phoned me. She said he's there now and has things under control."

"Very sensible." Smoothly Travis added, "Let me know if you need anything once you're back at the winery."

"Thanks. Sorry to eat and run. Have fun." Geilis threw Katy a wicked little wink and strode down the driveway to her car.

Moments later, Katy heard the squeal of tyres taking the corner onto the river road faster than was wise.

Adam ambled down the stairs, craning his head to see around the corner of the house. "Hey, isn't Geilis staying for dessert? I've brought out four slices of tart." He set a tray on the table and tipped his head. "Did she go?"

Katy handed a plate to Travis and one to Adam and took a plate for herself before taking her seat. "Her father had a bit of an accident and she's gone home to help."

"What happened?" Adam hoed into the citrus tart Katy had whipped up earlier.

One thing about Adam's appetite—it made her feel good

about her cooking ability. "Some boxes fell on Mr Romney and he might have a broken arm. That's why Geilis had to leave."

"Oh. Can I have her slice then? It's too good to waste." Adam's spoon scraped the last of his serving from his plate and he looked at Katy with a pitiful expression. "You wouldn't want to see me starve, would you?"

"What if Travis feels the same way?"

Adam blinked as though the thought hadn't occurred to him as he looked from Travis to the extra slice of citrus tart. "Would you like the slice, Travis?"

"Hmm, it was really delicious." Travis reached for the fourth plate, stopped short and looked at Adam.

Her nephew's face fell, but to his credit, he said nothing.

Travis grinned his lop-sided grin and slowly drew his hand back. "But you know what—I think I'd better watch my waistline. All yours, Adam, if—"

Adam already held the plate six inches off the tray. He froze, eyes wide as he waited for Travis to play out his little scene. "If—what?"

He was so good with Adam, and Katy regretted the snarky comments and their several little spats. Travis had been nothing but decent since her first incursion onto his property. She was lucky he was her neighbour. And maybe they were becoming friends. Stifling the desire to be more, to ask for more than he offered, she licked the last of the tart off the back of her spoon. It really was good, if she said so herself.

"If you'll agree to put in the time to learning backing guitar for a song at the Christmas concert we're organising. It will be hard work, but—"

"You want *me* to play with you?" Adam's voice cracked and the deeper tone of the voice he would grow into broke through his awed question. "Shit, yeah." He flicked a glance at Katy. " Sorry, I meant, gosh, yeah. Do you want to start now? I'll get my guitar. I promise I'll practise every day."

"Tomorrow is soon enough. Though maybe you could help Katy some more and do the washing up while we talk about plans for the concert."

"Sure. I'll eat this in the kitchen." Adam grabbed the dirty plates and cutlery and set his treasured second helping beside the stack on the tray and disappeared up the back stairs and into the kitchen.

"Nicely done." Katy picked up her glass and drank.

"He's a good kid. So, I've lined up several friends—their names are on this list." He handed the folder to her, but covered her hand with his before she could open it.

She looked into his eyes.

He turned his head slightly to the left but he met her gaze. An ache started in the region of her heart and she rubbed a knuckled fist over it. Was he still trying to hide his scar? Occasionally grumpy and definitely prickly, Travis had been kind to Adam and to her—once he'd got over her trespassing on Thornyhill land. In his gruff way he cared about people and yet he seemed unsure of his welcome.

Because of his scar? Did he think he was some hideous beast hiding away in his castle on the hill?

"Katy?"

She blinked and realised she'd zoned out briefly. "What was that?" Nerves and long-held dreams of Travis tied her tongue in knots as he moved closer and his hazel eyes darkened. In their depths her own desire was reflected. Tension, anticipation, hope—a cocktail of powerful emotions gripped her heart until she couldn't breathe. Dimly aware of his hand on hers, his thumb brushed back and forth in languid butterfly strokes on the sensitive skin of her wrist.

"Can I kiss you?"

If this was a dream she was going to enjoy every single moment before she woke.

She nodded once and leaned forward, meeting him halfway. "I'd like that."

"Me too." Lips brushed hers in a kiss as soft as a butterfly's wing.

The warmth of the night paled beside the heat of his broad chest so close to her. And yet, he hadn't touched her with anything more than his lips and one hand. Her heart glided like skaters across a moonlit pond as she closed her eyes and every sense concentrated on imprinting Travis' kiss into her memory. Leaning forward, she met an answering pressure as his mouth moved against hers.

Tentatively she ran her tongue along the seam of his lips. There, a hint of citrus when her tongue touched the corner of his mouth.

Scents of sandalwood rose around them and his fingers tunnelled into her hair, tipping her head back a little more.

"Katy." Her name was a ghost of sound, a whisper on the wind, a vibration of lips against lips. And it roared with need and want and desire inside her.

"Katy?" Adam's voice reached her across space and time and the darkness of the backyard. "Mum's on my phone and asking for you."

Katy reluctantly pulled away from Travis' lips and slowly opened her eyes. She blinked and drew what felt like her first breath in forever. "I'm coming." Travis grinned and she realised her words hadn't carried beyond him. They'd been breathy and laden with another meaning. She swallowed as a different heat crept up her cheeks, cast a final look at Travis' mouth and met his gaze.

Raising her voice and turning towards the house, she tried again. "I'll be right there."

As she swung her legs over the bench and took a step away from the table, away from Travis and the heady joy of his kisses, he took hold of her hand. "Don't be long, will you? We have a lot more to—discuss."

With more courage than she'd felt in a long time, she cupped his cheek and dropped a kiss on his mouth. It was meant to be quick, to be a promise of more to come, but her lips clung to his until Adam called for her again from the back landing.

"Are you coming, Katy? Mum said it's costing her heaps to phone from Japan."

Katy released Travis' lips and stood. "I'll be quick as I can; you can count on me. I don't want you disappearing just yet."

***

As Travis watched Katy cross the yard and climb the back stairs peace settled in his soul. All it had taken was a kiss from Katy and he felt like a new man. He could conquer mountains, ford rivers . . . write an album of songs for her, about her. He could achieve anything, and all things were possible because Katy had kissed him. He'd felt the desire simmering between them, burned with the heat of their attraction.

Katy kissed me. Wholeheartedly, passionately despite what I am.

He swung his legs over the bench and sat, elbows resting behind him on the table so he could see her as soon as she emerged from the house. So he could watch her returning to him.

Beside him, Katy's phone vibrated against his arm. He picked it up intending only to move it away from the edge of the table. He didn't intend to read the message, didn't mean to do more than rescue it from imminent descent to the concrete slab. But the night was dark and the screen was bright and the words burned into his brain.

Offer increased to $20,000 IF you deliver Travis Roberts. Aislinn.

Time stopped.

He'd thought the saying ridiculous, unrealistic hyperbole. As though a mere mortal event could stop time and shred the fabric of existence. And yet—and yet, nothing moved around him. His lungs stopped pumping, his heart ceased beating as though snap-frozen.

Cold enveloped Travis' heart as his vision narrowed on the bright yellow rectangle of light spilling from the kitchen. A shadow passed across the lower pane, breaking the spell cast by the message and he imagined Katy pacing and talking to her sister, telling her how clever she'd been, how she'd found an easy way to get the money for her renovation. How easily she'd duped him, Travis Roberts, the singing sensation from Lark Creek, into believing she didn't care about his scars. That she cared about him!

He was an idiot; a gullible fool to have thought Katy was different. He should have known the day she trespassed on his land—surely he had known—but there were none so blind as those who chose not to see.

I don't want you disappearing just yet.

His gaze swung to the driveway as headlights turned into Katy's property. Was this the television crew arriving to catch him off guard?

He tossed the phone into the centre of the table, pushed to his feet as though the weight of Lark Creek in full flood pushed against him. Gut churning, he strode from the pergola down the dark creek side of the house.

How could I have been so stupid? She'd told him, repeatedly, how much she needed money to renovate her grandmother's house. That money was to come from the sacrificial lamb in her plans. Him!

How could I have been so wrong about her?

"Damn you, Katy Leonard, you and your lying lips. You think you've got me sewn up in your little television episode, well think again." Fuelled by his anger and disappointment and hurt, his words slipped into the night, heard only by a restless magpie lark that flapped past him.

Wishing he was astride his motorbike instead of the quad bike, he stopped at the corner where Leonard Drive met the river road and glanced left, towards the winery. If Rick had needed his help he would have phoned by now. A slow burn started in his gut. Betrayal tasted like citrus tart—and Katy Leonard's lips.

Chapter Twenty-Eight

Katy ended the call to her sister and handed Adam's phone back.

Adam shoved the phone into his pocket and turned to fill the electric kettle at the sink. "Katy, a ute just pulled up in the driveway. Looks like Travis' ute but I know he rode his quad bike down."

The sound of boots ascending the back steps distracted her as a motorbike spun its wheels at the bottom of the road. She jumped as two sharp raps sounded on the back door. "I'll see who it is while you put the kettle on." Hoping whoever it was didn't delay her from getting back to Travis, she rounded the table, heading for the back door.

Travis—he'd kissed her once and the promise of more had been on his lips when she'd left him. Holding that memory, she opened the screen door.

Surprise wiped out her smile. She felt it melting away and quickly stepped outside, pushing the door closed behind her. "Rick? What are you doing here? Is Reg okay?"

"Sorry I had to call in. Travis isn't answering his phone and Reg Romney's wife asked me to give him an urgent message."

"Travis is at the table in the pergola. What's happened?"

"He's been taken to hospital. Paramedics reckon he has a broken arm and possible concussion." Rick turned and crossed to the railing and looked towards the structure.

Katy followed, her gaze seeking Travis. The light from the hurricane lamp looked cheerful and festive as it shone across the bright tablecloth, glinted off glasses and competed with the pink and blue Chinese lanterns strung along one side. The whole setting looked pretty and inviting. And empty. There was no Travis.

Her stomach took a dive and she gripped the railing. An unexpected sense of impending doom clutched at her throat. They'd kissed and she'd promised not to be gone long when Adam had called her. Travis had promised to wait—hadn't he? "Maybe he walked down towards the creek."

Rick frowned. "Okay. I'll go look. I really need to talk to him."

Casting a disbelieving look at the empty pergola, Katy hurried behind Rick. "I'll come with you." There was no sign of Travis along the side of the house, and when they reached the front gate, she stopped and looked at the empty grass footpath.

Rick ran a hand through his short, dark hair and turned back to her. "The quad's gone. It was parked outside when I pulled into your driveway. That's why I stopped. Sorry to have bothered you."

"It's fine. I—I don't know what's happened to him, but tell him I'll drop by in the morning, will you?"

"Sure." With no more social niceties, Rick headed to the ute—Travis' ute—and backed out, turning up Leonard Drive for the longer route back to Thornyhill Farm.

Adam had been right about the vehicle. If only she knew why Travis had left. Had she overwhelmed him with her enthusiasm for his kiss? The magpie larks called from their nest down near the creek, their two-note duet familiar as she headed for the pergola. There was no point in sitting outside any longer now Travis had gone. The light was much better in the kitchen, and Adam might want company. She didn't feel like spending the evening alone, not yet. Later she'd think about Travis' kiss.

But there was work to do before then.

She collected the last of the glasses and added them to the tray, picked up the folder Travis had set at one end of the table and her phone and turned off the lamp. Carefully she picked her way across the yard and manoeuvred her way one-handed through the screen door. From Adam's bedroom, the sounds of one of Travis' songs floated along the hallway. Snatches of chorus repeated as though on a loop.

Smiling to herself—Adam's connection with Travis was another wonderful result of reconnecting with her idol—she unloaded the tray and rinsed the glasses before settling down to peruse the information Travis had given to her.

Her phone chirped, the signal for a missed message, and she reached for the greeny-gold phone. Maybe it was from Travis explaining his sudden departure. She thumbed the button and stared at the message.

The *second* notification of a message.

"Shit."

She dragged in a breath and hit speed dial. If Travis had seen that message when it arrived, she was screwed.

The drawcard of a famous name. But she'd never use him like that. Never allow the media vultures to circle while she had breath in her body. He had to know that. He must.

"Come on, pick up, pick up please."

"You've reached Travis Roberts. Leave a message after the tone . . ."

Travis glared at the screen flashing Katy's name and clenched the phone in his left hand. The desire to hurl the flashing screen into the night was powerful. Instead, he raised the glass in his right hand and tossed back a shot of tequila. It burned in the back of his throat, a welcome burn that suited his mood rather too well. Not since the doctor had told him there was nerve damage in his right hand that might never repair itself had he felt so angry with himself.

Was he the most gullible fool on the planet to have believed Katy?

Headlights cut through the darkness and moments later Rick drove Travis' ute past the house to the garage. A car door slammed and Travis refilled his glass and poured a shot for Rick.

"Trav, where are you?"

"On the veranda." As Rick pushed through the front screen door, Travis held a glass out to him. "Let's have a toast—"

Rick took the glass and raised it. "What are we toasting?"

"Lying lips. *Skol.*" He tossed back the shot and stared into the darkness. There was another twist to the song that wouldn't—

couldn't—be written. But at least now he knew the reason why he was *missing* those lips. They had been a promise, a hope that his accident hadn't redefined him as a man and as a musician. The promise he might find someone who would see past his scars and want him for who he was.

"I'm glad you're here, Rick. There're a few things we should focus on tomorrow—"

"Trav, about tomorrow. Jillian Romney asked if I'd consider helping out at the winery. Reg has damaged his arm. I said I would."

"Of course. You need to go. Mate, that's a positive step for you. Working at the winery will help you ease your way back into the community, show them that others trust you."

"Reg and Jillian trust me and that's a start."

"It's a great start having them on your side." Belatedly Travis registered that Rick hadn't included Geilis in his trust circle.

"Sorry to desert you so soon after I arrived. But the Romneys need me. I can't let Jill down."

Travis poured another shot into their glasses and raised it to his friend. "You're a good man, Rick. Here's to others learning what I've always known." He tapped his glass against Rick's and downed the shot.

Rick leaned back against the railing and fixed Travis with a searching look. "Why did you leave Rose Cottage so suddenly? Your quad was out front when I pulled into the driveway and when I went around the front of the house, you were gone. What happened?"

"That was you?" A sinking feeling in his gut had nothing to do with tequila shots and everything to do with terrible timing. But the fact that it had been Rick and not the television crew didn't alter the evidence. The message on Katy's phone revealed she was playing some deeper game with him as the prize. "I left because I thought you were the television crowd arriving."

"Fat chance. Katy seemed surprised you'd left."

"I hope she—"

What did he hope? Until Rick had returned, he'd almost

wished she lost the chance to be part of the renovation show. But then she'd have to sell her grandmother's house and leave Lark Creek for good. He wouldn't wish that loss on anyone. Rose Cottage was Katy's last link to her grandmother and to her father. He knew better than many what it was like to lose what was most precious to him.

After the thrill of her kisses, it would take him a long time to get over Katy's betrayal.

"I'm going out to check on Samson." Maybe in his current frame of mind, he'd be better company for the lonely little donkey than for Rick. "I'll see you in the morning before you go."

Hands in pockets he strolled down to the stables and switched on the low wattage night light. Samson stood with his nose in the corner, his back turned on the world. A strange affinity with the donkey filled Travis and he eased slowly and cautiously into the stall until he could lower his hand where the donkey could see and smell him.

Samson turned his head away and lowered it, appearing defeated, but shutting Travis out the only way he could. Kind of like how Travis had been shutting out the world, both nursing scars on their faces that were seared into their souls.

He rested a hand on Samson's head. The donkey flinched and anger welled in Travis. Someone had harmed the poor creature until even a simple touch filled him with fear. Travis began a gentle, slow stroking on the donkey's head and kept his tone soft and soothing. "It's okay, fella, I won't hurt you. I'll look after you and maybe one day you'll feel safe enough to stick your nose out into the big wide world outside."

Chapter Twenty-Nine

Katy gripped her phone and closed her eyes against the bright sunlight reflecting off the sliver of creek through the trees. "Thanks for your offer, Aislinn, but there is no way I'm going to ask an unwilling participant to be on your show just to get money to renovate my grandmother's home." Tired of politely telling the presenter to get stuffed, she hoped Aislinn understood her refusal this time around.

"Okay, your loss. Without Travis Roberts, the station is opting out of your property. That's the official word. But Katy—" Aislinn's voice dropped to a softer level and the noise in the background was muffled as though she'd moved into a different, private space. "Privately, I'd like to say, good on you. Your *Sam* is lucky to have you watching out for him. Good luck." The connection was cut and Katy sat looking at her phone in disbelief.

Well, there was one person who approved of her decision. If only she hadn't left her phone beside Travis, maybe she'd have had him on her side too. He had to have seen that message and felt a twinge of nerves about her plans.

Twenty thousand twinges.

But he wasn't taking her calls and he hadn't answered his door when she rode up to the house this morning. If his ute hadn't been missing, she'd have thought he was avoiding her. But the more she thought about his sudden departure, the angrier she became.

What about fair play and listening to an explanation? What about even asking what I intended to do instead of assuming I'm guilty?

Given no chance to explain stung the most of all. It was so reminiscent of her mother's reactionary approach to parenting. Any problem, any infraction of McMansion rules and Katy had copped the blame. No questions, just a sad face and put-upon attitude of *Look what I must endure* from her mother.

Gripping the railing, she barely saw the car pull into her

driveway. "Stuff you, Travis Roberts. Someone else can deal with your tantrums."

But it was Rick Peyton who climbed out of the driver's seat. He made no move to approach, but stood beside the open door. "Travis is out of town until the concert. He said his manager will be in touch about the details." He put one foot back inside the car.

"Wait! Is that it?"

Rick looked up from beneath hooded eyes. "That's the message. I've got to get to work." He climbed in before she had a chance to ask where Travis had gone, reversed out of her driveway and turned left along the river road.

Adam came out of the house and stood beside her, bare-chested and tousle-haired in a pair of long pyjama pants. He yawned and stretched and ran his fingers through his hair, making more spikes in it. "He doesn't look the type."

"And just what *type* would that be? You can't tell what people are really like just by looking at them." Looking at Travis, she wouldn't have picked him for a judgemental prick, but his actions said otherwise.

Adam shrugged. "Do you know what time Travis wants me to go up for my lesson?"

Like a hand around her throat, Adam's question stole her breath. Travis had promised lessons to Adam, had invited him to play guitar. Had he forgotten, or did he really care so little for others that he'd disappoint a vulnerable teenager? "I—don't know. Why don't you text him and ask?"

Maybe Travis would respond to Adam even if he refused to speak to her. Besides, if he was going to blow off her nephew, it was better it came from him. Why should she wear the backlash? Except she probably would.

"Okay. Do you want a coffee?"

"Sure, thanks."

As she waited for Adam to return, the issue of Travis' reneging on his promise to Adam gnawed at her until, unable to resist, she pulled her phone from the pocket of her shorts and typed a message:

Don't take out how you feel about me on Adam. Please.

She hit the send button and tossed her phone on the table. Right now she had better things to think about than Travis Roberts.

She had a concert to help co-ordinate and a job to find.

***

Travis' phone pinged again. He almost deleted the message without reading, but Adam's name caught his eye.

Damn. In all this mess the teenager was an innocent victim. He wouldn't abandon Adam, no matter how much he didn't want to see Katy again. And yet, if he were honest, that was only partly true. Maybe she had succumbed to the lure of the money offered by the television station, but she'd done her best to see her nephew made reparation for his vandalism, and probably out of her own pocket. Maybe things really were so tight for her she'd felt she had no option. It still didn't excuse her choice to cast him to the wolves, but . . .

The idea struck him suddenly and from out of nowhere. Kyle had bemoaned the costs of grabbing airtime on the local television channel. What if he, Travis, were to agree to appear on Katy's episode? Could they leverage that for some free publicity?

His gut churned at the thought. Worse than performing on stage, was he really considering appearing on TV? The idea of his face in close up created spasms that rippled through his stomach and threatened to expel his breakfast. But if he was serious about participating in the country Christmas concert, there would be phones videoing him anyway. They would be completely outside his control, whereas he could make certain stipulations to the program manager.

Before he could change his mind, he hit the speed dial for Kyle's number and waited for his manager to pick up.

"Yo, Trav, what's up now?"

Travis swallowed the bile that rose in his throat at the

thought of what he was about to do. "Kyle, this doesn't mean I'm not still mad about Katy's deceit, but we could use my appearing on that renovation show to ask for free publicity of the Christmas concert. What do you think?"

"Bloody brilliant, mate. I'll get onto it now."

"Kyle? Only if they agree to a couple of requests. I'm emailing them through to you now."

Chapter Thirty

Katy watched in disbelief as the television van turned into her driveway and Aislinn opened the door closest to the kitchen window. With a hand that trembled more than she liked, Katy smoothed her hair and tucked her shirt into her jeans before she went outside to greet the presenter.

"I don't understand what changed your mind about taking on my project. This change from no-go to full throttle has come out of the blue. I thought you were clear that I won't—can't—offer up Travis Roberts."

Aislinn gave her a strange, narrow-eyed look and accepted the microphone from one of the crew. "I get that, Katy. It's all sorted—apparently. Now, what I need you to do is be ready to answer your front door when I knock. We'll film the meeting from both sides, one after the other, so you'll have to try to remember exactly what you do and say when we do the second take. Okay?"

"Okay. God, I'm so nervous."

Aislinn touched Katy's arm and smiled. "You'll be fine. Just look at me, not at the camera, and follow my lead. See you at your front door."

Sweaty hands were the least of her worries. She had a quick drink of water to moisten her dry mouth. Why was it that coming to Lark Creek had forced her into speaking in public more often than ever before in her life? Lifting her chin and pinning a smile in place, she stood in front of the closed door, hand ready to turn the knob.

A firm trio of knocks sounded. Katy took a deep breath and opened the door. Her breath whooshed out, her jaw dropped and she just barely managed to stay upright.

Travis stood in front of her with a camera peering over his right shoulder.

***

He wasn't sure if this was the best way to admit his mistake, but Katy couldn't refuse to hear his apology. Not with a camera aimed at the two of them. But when her eyes lighted on him her smile evaporated like summer mist burned off by the heat of the sun. Her cheeks paled and then flared with colour and he wondered if he'd made a monumental mis-assessment.

"Hi, Katy, I thought I'd drop by to see how your renovations are going." Words that didn't belong to him, that had been scripted for him by some anonymous writer fell flat on their face before Katy's withering glare.

"Really?"

"And cut." Aislinn appeared behind Travis. "Katy, can you give us some pleasure at seeing Travis?"

"Why? I've spent the past few days trying to contact him without so much as an *I'm listening* from him and you want me to pretend to be joyful now?"

Travis turned his head with a grimace. "Told you springing this on Katy wasn't a good idea. Let me talk to her alone and then— well, we'll take it from there."

"Remember our agreement, Travis."

"Yeah, how can I forget? Just—can you give us a few minutes to sort this out?" He stepped inside with difficulty. Katy seemed rooted to the spot. Either that, or she was so angry with him, she had no intention of letting him inside.

He closed the door behind him and looked at Katy. "I really am sorry, Katy. This was their idea to surprise you. I told Aislinn it wasn't a good idea, that you don't like being the centre of attention at the best of times, but—"

Katy backed away and folded her arms. Her gaze would have turned him to stone under other circumstances. As it was, he'd made it inside.

"What *agreement?* Aislinn said to remember your *agreement.*"

This was what he should have explained to her before the television crew arrived, before a camera was shoved in her face. No, actually he should have given her the apology she richly deserved first

179

and without an audience looking on. His stomach clenched as he realised how badly he'd handled—everything. His gaze dropped to her mouth, to the lips that had inspired his return to the land of the living.

Focus, Roberts. There's more than a mere show at stake here. This is about your future.

"In the spirit of getting as much free publicity as possible for our concert, I offered to appear on your episode of the renovation show if the station agreed to support our Christmas concert with a free fifteen second ad attached to every airing of the promo for your project. As myself, not as your mythical *Sam.*" He waited for light to dawn, for Katy to at least acknowledge she understood what this was costing him in emotional energy.

Her shoulders hunched and her chin rose higher. "Big of you. Why do you think I want you on my reno episode? What makes you think I still want to do the show anyway?"

"The fact you need money to go ahead." She was pricklier than he'd ever seen her. Not that he would complain, if only she'd agree to go on with the show. Step one in making things up to Katy; ensure she got the money to do up Rose Cottage so she could stay in Lark Creek.

After that, step two was . . . There was no point getting ahead of himself.

"But I don't want to go ahead. I told them that after they offered me an obscene amount of money to con you into appearing. If you hadn't run off into the night, I'd have shared that tidbit with you the night of our barbecue. As it is, I no longer care."

"You still need a cash flow to make your renovation work. This show will give it to you. You could be open in time for the Christmas concert crowd."

"I backed off, Travis, because I'd rather wait and earn my own money than sell my soul to get theirs. I've decided I don't want to be in front of the camera so you can just go out there and tell them there is no deal, other than whatever you want to cut with them."

He held out a hand, intending only to touch her shoulder, but she took a step backwards and smacked into the wall. Instead, he held both hands up to show her he wouldn't touch her again. Despite her occasional self-doubt, Katy could be a tough customer when she was determined on a course of action. But he wouldn't let her suffer for his stupidity. "Look, I get that you're annoyed with me, but think of the good it could do for our town. This concert could be the beginning of its recovery. The station pays you for bringing me on board, and they donate invaluable airtime to promote our event to potential visitors. This way, we both get what we want, and Lark Creek benefits."

He didn't want to crowd her, didn't want her to feel under pressure, but she had to see how important a part she had to play. "Katy, if it hadn't been for you, none of this would be happening in the first place. Without you, I would still be holed up in the house on the hill. How can you refuse to a part of the biggest thing to happen in Lark Creek in years?"

Adam appeared from the direction of the kitchen and looked from Travis to Katy. "Come on, Katy. If you don't do this stupid show, the concert might not go ahead. And then how will I live it down?"

"Live what down?"

"I told my mates I'm going to be playing on stage with Travis. I'll never be able to go back to school and look them in the eye again if the concert doesn't happen. Please, Katy?"

"Please, Katy?" Travis couldn't put it any more eloquently or simply than had Adam. "You have my apology for acting more of an ass than Samson. I can't promise not to have another freak-out; only that I'll try to let you know that it's happening rather than lashing out like I have done. But Katy, I really want us to do this together."

"The TV show?"

"Bring Lark Creek back to life. Because I think—I hope we might have a future here—together. Will you give us a chance, give me another chance?"

She blinked as tears filled her eyes and raised a hand to his damaged cheek. "For Gran's sake—and for us."

Her touch was light, but he swore his damaged cheek felt it. And then she stepped close and tipped her face up to his. "I've always liked the idea of second chances."

Vaguely aware of movement to his left, Travis didn't care. He lowered his head and claimed Katy's lips for his own. Lips he had missed for far too long.

Chapter Thirty-One

Sunlight caught the gold highlights and the dewdrop artistically resting on the painted rose as Katy stepped back and looked at the sign. '*Rose Cottage B & B*' was picked out in red and gold letters with fine black shadowing. Travis' builder friend, Fergus shovelled in the last spadeful of cement holding the post and checked the supports before he stood and joined her and the signwriter, Anna.

Katy clasped her hands together and looked from the builder to the artist. "Thanks, Fergus. Gran would have loved this, Anna. You've done a beautiful job of the writing and image. Thank you."

The artist-cum-signwriter took out a soft cloth and ran it over the pristine sign one last time. "My pleasure. I'm glad you like the design. It seemed to suit what you told me about your grandmother, and it certainly suits the rose garden she created." She collected the packaging in which the sign had been wrapped while Fergus packed his tools into the back of his van, the one that looked similar to the television crew's vehicle and that had confused Travis several weeks earlier.

"I really appreciate both of you fitting in my job when I know how busy you are in the lead up to Christmas."

Anna touched her arm and smiled. "It was my pleasure. I think it's lovely what you're doing here."

"Thanks."

"No worries, Katy. When Travis told me what kind of crazy schedule you were trying to meet and how important it was to you to have everything finished before you scatter your gran's ashes, well, I couldn't refuse, either planting the post or working on the house. You've done a fantastic job both in the garden and in the renovation."

"Thanks, Fergus. You've been a marvel." Her gaze flicked across to the rosebush and she sighed softly. "I guess I should get ready. The others will be arriving for the ceremony very soon. See you at the concert on Saturday." She hurried up the stairs and into the house.

The cherry-red summer dress she'd bought especially for today was on a hanger on the outside of her wardrobe. Gran had always loved bright colours, and it seemed fitting to farewell her in the brightest, boldest colour Katy could find. After a quick shower, she stepped into the slim-fitting dress and, looking at herself in the full-length cheval mirror, smoothed the fabric over her hips.

I can do this.

The urn stood on the mantelpiece where it had sat since the night of Katy's return to Lark Creek. She touched the pagoda-shaped wooden lid and drew a deep breath before she picked up the urn. Clutching it to her chest as she walked slowly towards the front door, her fingers locked in place.

I can't do this. I can't say goodbye to Gran like this. Not here, not now, not ever.

Opening the urn and scattering her ashes was too final. It was an ending on the day of a new beginning for Rose Cottage. It was wrong, so very wrong. Her breathing was choppy as she shook her head.

A motor being turned off drew her gaze to the street where Geilis pulled up beside Travis' newly repaired motorbike. Bessie was already seated beside Adam on the garden bench in the new arbour Katy had installed, angled towards the creek.

Gran's friends—her friends. They were here to support Katy, and to say their own goodbyes. Travis stood at the bottom of the front stairs looking up at her. He raised a hand in invitation, in support, and waited for her to come to him. Blinking back the tears that filled her eyes at the thought of saying goodbye, she descended the front steps, keeping her gaze on Travis framed by the archway over the front gate, the one Gran had charmed her husband into building for her so long ago.

Roses grew in profusion, climbing the arch and blooming in

long trailing stems that swayed in the soft breeze. In the week before Christmas and the concert, it felt right and auspicious to have such prolific flowering for the unveiling of the sign and the opening of Katy's B & B.

And for saying goodbye to Gran.

Katy and Travis joined the small circle—Geilis, Bessie, Adam trying to unobtrusively film the ceremony for his mother—as they stood around Gran's favourite rosebush. Several deep-red blooms had opened with a number of buds at varying stages of opening filling in the spaces between. The air was redolent with a heady sweet fragrance and the petals were soft on her skin as she stroked the nearest bloom.

Her gaze fell on each person in the circle before she spoke. "Thank you all for coming—for being here and sharing this moment with us—with me. Gran was dear to all of us and a wonderful friend and support in tough times. I loved her deeply and I will miss her every day of my life. But I know she'll never be far from me, not now. Each of you has shown me, in your own way, that those we love don't ever truly leave us. They live on in our hearts, and in our memories."

She looked around the small circle of faces. "Would anyone like to say a few words before—"

Bessie nodded. "Merle was a dear, dear friend. For over sixty years she was there for me; a shoulder to lean on, a friendly ear, the warmth and trust of a beautiful soul. And I know she's here with us still. I feel her presence—it's in the love within this group, in the bones of this home she made and in the garden she created from nothing."

A tremble passed through Katy. It was time.

Travis rested a hand on the small of her back. Light as it was, his touch grounded her, reminded her she wasn't alone in missing her grandmother. That she wasn't alone.

Fingers trembling only a little, Katy turned the lid of the urn and dropped it onto the grass beside her. As the little group looked on she gently, reverently tipped the ashes into the small circular trough around the red rose. Gran would never leave her. She would be here in her beloved garden forever, looking out over the terrace and the creek.

As she tipped the urn completely upside down the wind caught the last of the fine ash and carried it towards the creek along with Katy's silent farewell.

Goodbye, Gran. I love you.

Epilogue
Christmas Eve Country Christmas Round Up

The crowd in front of Rory Donovan's flat trailer was even bigger than they'd hoped. It had grown steadily through the afternoon as a stream of Australia's finest answered Travis' call. One after another, well-known performers had taken to the stage, enthralling audiences with the array of Aussie country talent. But everyone knew the real drawcard was Travis. His return to performance after his accident would have drawn a huge crowd even if the heavens opened, as they'd been threatening to do all week.

The emcee stepped up to the microphone and the crowd edged closer. "You lot know who's up next, don't you?" A wave of anticipation rose from the crowd, along with a lot of hands holding cans of beer aloft. "I could make you wait a while longer with a long intro about how amazing it is to have the king of country back performing for us—"

"Get orf the stage."

"Bring out Travis."

"Tra-vis, Tra-vis." More and more voices picked up the chant and the emcee grinned.

"Please welcome back Lark Creek's own son and Aussie singing legend, Travis Roberts." A roar of excitement almost overwhelmed the drummer's introduction as Travis walked out onto the stage and waved to the crowd. Clapping and whistling and multiple flashes from a myriad of phone cameras didn't faze him.

From behind the fenced off side of the trailer, Katy straightened Adam's collar as he looked at her. "Katy, what if I stuff up?" Nerves had kicked in and Adam's cheeks were pale beneath the tan of several weeks in the country.

Katy squeezed his shoulder and smiled at him. "You've practised every day for weeks. You know the music back to front and inside out. And if I can face a crowd and speak by myself, I have every confidence you'll play brilliantly in Travis' band. Ready? Deep breath. Now smile—go and do us and yourself proud."

Adam joined the band surrounding Travis, and plugged in the lead the bass player handed him. Travis shot him a smile, turned back to the audience and strummed one long, loud chord. A cheer rose as he launched into the highway song that was still one of Katy's favourites.

She clasped her hands together as her gaze shifted from Travis to Adam and back. She was so proud of Adam, and so grateful to Travis for all he'd given to her nephew. The song finished to thunderous applause and the cameras panned over the crowd before returning to Travis. Aislinn and a small crew had exclusive rights to film the concert and Travis had suggested donating the money to a fighting fund to revitalise the town.

He played several more songs from earlier albums with his band, and then the spotlight narrowed on him and the rest of the stage dimmed.

He stepped up to his microphone and tucked his guitar to one side. "Thank you for your warm welcome home. There's something I'd like to do now, to say thank you. Thanks to all of you for supporting our first Christmas in the Country concert. Will you be back next Christmas?"

A roar of approval greeted his question.

Travis played up to it by tilting his head and holding his right ear towards them as he asked, "I didn't hear you. Will you be here next year?"

Katy hadn't thought it was possible but the sound doubled and rose like a promise into the moonlit sky.

"Great, 'cos I'll be here next year. But you know, none of this would have happened without one very brave and amazing woman. This next song is for her—for you, Katy Leonard."

Katy gasped. What was he doing? What song was he going to sing for her?

He turned and gave her a lopsided smile that melted her heart and warmed her from head to toe. The intro began, an unfamiliar tune that was different from Travis' other work. More ballad than anything else. And then he sang—about the girl that he missed and her lips that he'd kissed.

A small spotlight picked out Katy at the side of the stage, but she barely noticed. Her attention was totally on Travis. On the song he'd written about her. For her.

A love song.

Katy nestled her head on Travis' shoulder, pointed the remote at his television and turned it off. She wriggled her hips closer and thanked whoever had chosen his lounge chair for choosing one that accommodated two people with ease. "I never expected to be on TV making out with you."

"Neither did I, but you were a natural at it."

"Very funny. I didn't even notice they were filming us when you kneeled down at the edge of that stage."

"Do you mind? I mean, they got my bad side and I do mean *bad*."

"Travis Roberts, you don't have a bad side."

"Tell that to my manager. He's insisting all future promo shots include my scar. It's apparently now part of my brand." He leaned down and kissed her with just enough sense of urgency that she regretted inviting several friends to a bonfire party. It would have been nice to spend the evening kissing Travis under the starry skies.

Kyle stuck his head around the kitchen doorway. "Did someone just take my name in vain?"

Travis pegged a cushion at him. "Aren't you supposed to be looking after the bonfire and supervising Adam?"

"Man, he's fine. He's sharpened enough sticks for marshmallows to feed an army."

Katy giggled and pushed to her feet. "Honestly, I should go and keep him company. See you out there in a few minutes?"

"Sure. We'll be the ones with the giant packets of marshmallows."

As she walked through the kitchen, Kyle leaned against the doorframe. "I seem to recall a certain bet made between we two that a certain singer songwriter would sing the song inspired by his muse at the Christmas concert. Katy, I may need your help to make said singer pay up."

"Don't look at me, Kyle. My work is done. You don't know how tiring it is to be—" Feeling giddy with confidence, she struck a melodramatic pose. "—a singer's muse. I need sugar. I need marshmallows." She grabbed one of the packets from the bench and, giggling, escaped through the screen door.

The other guests were playing a game with torches in the back field as Katy reached the barn. She could wait for her marshmallows until they finished. A mournful bray cut through the night and she pushed open the barn door. Samson stood in his corner stall, a solitary figure that even Travis hadn't been able to coax outside. She approached the little donkey and slowly reached a hand over the railing and scratched his head. At least he no longer stood all day with his head in the corner. The long scar down his nose was healing, but he'd always carry that mark of his mistreatment. "Hello, Samson. It's Christmas night and it would be so nice if you deigned to join us around the fire."

She opened the door of his stall, hoping against hope that he might venture outside on this night of all nights. "Don't you want to see how beautiful it is outside? I'll leave the door open, just in case you change your mind."

Slowly she wandered outside. Travis would be there soon, and maybe later, they would catch up on more of those kisses he claimed they'd missed out on. The barn door creaked and movement in the doorway caught her eye.

Katy stood by the bonfire, holding her breath and watching as Samson poked his long grey-brown nose through the barn door. He took a couple of steps out of the barn, then a couple more, as though drawn by the bonfire. Slowly, but steadily, the donkey approached until he stopped a few metres from the dancing flames. Entranced, Katy eased closer until she stood by his side and wrapped her arms around his neck.

***

Travis strolled towards the fire with a couple of beers in hand, grateful Katy had forgiven his boorish behaviour, grateful beyond measure she had answered his *I love you* in kind. As he rounded the end of the barn, the bonfire flared bright, illuminating two figures. He stopped and stared in wonder.

Samson.

Of all the things he'd expected to see this wasn't one of them. Katy's arms were around the donkey's neck and he stood quietly. No kicking, no sawing rusty-voiced complaints. Travis' throat tightened. He'd tried hard and long with Samson, but it was Katy with her brightness and light who'd brought Samson out of the barn and into her arms.

Like him. Katy had broken through his standoffish armour and sorry-for-himself attitude and brought him back into the glare of the public. His public. His scars would fade, but she wouldn't allow him to fade into the background. The Christmas event had seen to that. Fully televised on national television—with him centre stage.

Finally, he believed in miracles. Because Katy Leonard was his own personal Christmas angel—his forever muse.

The End

I hope you enjoyed your introduction to Lark Creek! If you would like to share the love and leave a review, I would be grateful.

Here's a sneak peek at **A Lark Creek Vintage** (book 2) – Rick and Geilis' story.

Chapter One

"Why?" Geilis Romney couldn't prevent her shock spilling from her lips in one explosive syllable.

Her father's eyes widened and he gripped the arm of the chair with his one good hand. "Why— as in why hire anyone to help you run the vineyard, or why hire Rick Peyton?"

Her mind grappled with the alternatives, neither of which pleased her. The first suggested arrogance on her part to expect her father to hand over total control, but the second . . . Why did the fact he'd chosen Rick bother her so much? "You asked me to step in and run the vineyard while you're recuperating and then you went behind my back and hired—someone. Damn it, of all people you could have hired, why Rick Peyton?"

"Geilis Maree Romney, never tell me you've caught the small-mindedness of some people around here? I'm disappointed that you *of all people*"—God she hated it when he copied her words in that tone of voice— "can't see the value in giving a man like Rick another chance now he's out of prison."

"But it's not—" Biting off the end of her response she turned and looked out over the sea of grape vines laden with nearly ripe bunches. Harvest time was fast approaching and the lack of rain had produced more intense sugar in the fruit, flavour she was certain would make their best vintage in several years.

Movement along the top row of vines caught her eye. Rick stopped near the end of the row and carefully raised a bunch of grapes. His dark head tipped first one way then the other as he examined the fruit from both sides.

Antipathy towards the hired help wouldn't make managing the family business any easier. Explaining her objections to her father was impossible when she didn't fully understand the why of it herself. It hurt that Dad believed her capable of such petty behaviour, but *why* did Rick's presence rattle her as it did?

Rick had unsettled her even before he was found guilty. Coming home from uni with some level of maturity and an oenology degree under her belt, the sight of him up a ladder clearing Merle Leonard's gutters had stolen Geilis' ability to think and to breathe. He was a good-looking man—make that more like a feast for her eyes—and the fact he was helping Merle in a neighbourly way for no pay shot his appeal sky-high. That first sight of him after several years away at uni had rocked her. Alarmed and shocked her. She and Katy might have ogled Travis Roberts' poster a time or three, but Geilis wasn't really interested in the singer. But Rick Peyton—he'd sent her temperature skyrocketing. But she couldn't—wouldn't—allow herself to be distracted.

Working with her father, Romney Wines was going to become one of Australia's top wineries and no man was going to come between her and her goal.

She hated Rick for the way she reacted around him and locked her attraction behind sarcastic comments and studied indifference. She hated him . . . even while her gaze zeroed in on his tall, lean frame and drank its fill. Her hands rose to cover her heated cheeks at the memory of Rick stripping off his T-shirt and dropping it from the top of the ladder. The sight of his toned body superimposed itself on the scene in front of her.

Damn the distraction and damn Rick for accepting the job here.

She turned back and faced her father. Morning light slanted through the east-facing window highlighting grey in his hair she'd never noticed before. Her heart thudded as she realised his shoulders had developed a stoop almost overnight. How could she add to his concerns by raising an issue that suddenly seemed less important than the fact Rick Peyton had the strength her father lacked but had tried to provide for her by hiring the man?

"It won't be a problem, Dad. Rick is here for a limited time as the muscle. When your arm has healed, he'll be gone and we'll be back to the way we were."

God, she hoped they could go back to the way they were.

***

Rick Peyton looked over the rows of grape vines angling down the slope towards Lark Creek and wondered what the hell he'd agreed to. White grapes hung in plump bunches on his left, and off to the right, heavy, dark purple orbs tempted him with the promise of pleasure. They looked ripe and ready for the picking, but what did he know about wine? Even before he'd been sent to prison he preferred an amber brew.

He shrugged and climbed onto the quad bike. Not that his taste in drink mattered. Thanks to Geilis' father, he had a job doing the heavy lifting at Romney wines. For an ex-con, landing a job was a big step.

Ex-con. Gritting his teeth, he tipped his head back and looked at the wide arc of open sky. Unimpeded by bars and wire, it disappeared beyond the far hill where he could make out Travis' house at Thornyhill farm. Below the edge of the vineyard, the creek meandered in a gentle curve. In the still summer air the sound of water tumbling over rocks at the bend below the vineyard carried to his ears. If he wanted to he could stroll down to the bank and spend as much time as he wanted just sitting and watching the creek. Toss in a stick, skim a few stones—*think*. No rules, no strictly regulated outside time—nothing but nature inviting him to disappear into the bush and sleep under the stars.

Six months jail time, six months behind bars and forever labelled a criminal—did my sacrifice achieve my goal?

He closed his eyes and drew in a deep lungful of air. The scent of earth and ripening fruit on the vine filled his nostrils. The scent of freedom.

"If you're going to daydream get off that quad bike and let me take the equipment to the lower section."

His eyelids flew open at Geilis' annoyed tone. Standing on the bluestone patio looking down at him, arms folded across her waist and a no-nonsense *hiring-you-was-a-mistake* expression in her eyes, she was all business. Her red-checked shirt was knotted at her waist and a pair of faded denims disappeared into the tops of her work boots. A battered, broad-brimmed hat lay on the ironwork table next to her. Clearly she intended to supervise him in the first task Reg had set for the day. The idea grated against his newfound freedom.

Suppressing the urge to respond came automatically. Passive face, hands otherwise engaged in gripping the steering wheel—he'd quickly learned the technique of *non-involvement* and avoided trouble in the exercise yard. Watching without appearing to look, heightened awareness of his surroundings, and most important of all, giving away nothing of his true feelings.

Let it slide like water off a duck's back.

"On my way." He turned the key in the ignition and released the brake as Geilis stepped off the flagged patio. Okay, so maybe he had been enjoying his freedom for a few moments before work began, but after six months behind bars—six months of his life in exchange for protecting those he loved—it had felt like a stolen luxury.

He was aware of Geilis glaring at him as he drove past her down the central crossroad separating the two halves of the vineyard. Glaring and annoyed and definitely not liking his presence on Romney land.

Because I'm an ex-con. I'd better get used to it. She won't be the only one.

And here's a taster of my Outback series, *Hearts of the Outback.*

Just One Kiss: http://bit.ly/1Oq3KAX

Chapter One

"The horses are at the barrier . . . and *they're off and racing* in the Cloncurry Stakes. Big Mike takes an early lead but the favourite, Jester, is . . ." The race caller's excited voice blurred amid cheers from the crowd thronging the remote north-west Queensland racecourse.

Dr Dan Middleton glanced at the red dirt track and the dust cloud lazily settling over the race day crowd. Women dressed as smartly as those at Flemington on Cup Day teetered on high heels on hard-packed earth. If there were a few more plastic cups of beer than flutes of champagne, the effect was much the same.

He swallowed the last of his beer and swatted at the flies hovering near his mouth. Horses thundered around the final bend and the crowd surged towards the barriers. A whirly-wind picked up dust, swirling and tracking behind a slim, young woman, the only other racegoer not focused on the race. Caught unawares by the sudden gust, she turned her back and struggled to hold her hat and dress as it lifted in the wind. Her pink dress ballooned and flipped up like one of his mother's fuschias. Tanned legs went all the way up to a pair of silky white panties and Dan grinned.

As suddenly as it had risen, the wind dropped. The woman exhaled and swatted dust from her full skirt. Twitching the outfit into place, she continued towards the beer tent. And Dan.

Faint pink flared in her cheeks as her gaze connected with his and he realised he was still ogling her and grinning.

"Perv." She pushed past him, knocking the plastic cup out of his hand.

By the time he retrieved it and stood, she had disappeared into the crowd around the bar.

"Great way to make an impression, doc." Mark Rogers, a mechanic with the Royal Flying Doctor Service in Mt. Isa, raised his cup in a mock salute.

"Bad timing. Story of my life." How could he have let himself forget the perils of showing his appreciation of the female form? Surely he'd learned that lesson by now?

"How so, doc? Thought you'd have nurses hanging off your arm. Besides, our Amy's a pretty girl and—"

"Drop it, Mark. Not interested." Dan couldn't afford to be. As much as his job with the Royal Flying Doctor Service let him follow his passion for rural medicine, like his mother and grandfather before him, it was an opportunity to get away from the mud slinging. Although he was pleased his staff at Gosford Hospital had told the truth and stood up for him. And now—

"Don't say that too loud. People might think you're—"

"Gay?" he finished off for the burly mechanic.

"So you're not interested in Amy? She'll be relieved to hear that."

"I'm here to work. That's all. Why?"

"You're rostered on together. She's your pilot."

##

Amy Alistair peered into the small mirror in the ladies loo. Dust caked her face and her cleavage itched, and her new dress had acquired an unflattering layer of red that even the drycleaner would struggle to remove.

And her last-in-the-field horse was probably still running, which was why she'd been heading to the beer tent when the willy-willy sent her skirt flying and Mr Smug and Brooding had copped an eyeful.

Along with half the male population of town.

He'd been the first male she encountered after the wind

caught her unawares, and maybe she'd overreacted but his amusement had ratcheted up her embarrassment and her temper had run away with her. Dull red had stained his cheeks as he bent to pick up the cup she'd knocked out of his hand.

She almost felt sorry for him. Until Mechanic Mark nudged him and nodded in her direction. Slinking behind two burly blokes propping up the bar, she sought a safe, non-windy corner where she could quietly sink into the floor. Thank goodness she'd be back in the Isa tomorrow and could get back into work trousers.

Sharyn, her nemesis at high school and all-round stuck-up prig since she'd won Miss North West Queensland, popped her head around the entrance and chuckled. "Hey, Amy, nice knickers. Didn't realise you were so hard up for a date that you'd flash everyone. But hey, you got the eye of the new hottie." With a snort, Sharyn waved her mobile phone and withdrew.

Damn the two-second rule. If Sharyn had seen Amy's awkward moment, the whole region would know by—Amy checked her watch—now.

Oh, hell, had Sharyn got photos too?

Amy cruised along the strip of highway back to the Isa, her iPod on shuffle. As her red ute crested a slight rise, the headlights caught on metallic silver paint and flashing hazard lights. She eased back on the accelerator and pulled in behind a car with its bonnet raised. Someone had left the races earlier than her, it seemed. And by the large dent in the bonnet, they'd encountered a roo on the highway back to Mt. Isa.

She switched her lights to low beam and stepped out of her ute. The driver appeared around the front of the car, holding a torch in one hand and shading his eyes with the other.

"Well, if that doesn't put the icing on this day." She bit her lip, hoping her muttered comment hadn't carried to the man.

"Thanks for stopping. I've lost a headlight and—" Mr Smug and Brooding stopped as she walked past the front of her car. Of course it had to be him broken down at the side of the road. She contemplated jumping back in her ute and hightailing it. For all of five seconds.

"Yeah, well, let's see how bad the damage is." Even to her own ears, her voice sounded snarky. But dammit, she'd bought a new dress and that stupid hat and even crammed her feet into high heels for the racing carnival in celebration of her promotion.

Stupid choice. When did any male look at Amy Alistair with more than friendship on his mind? She was one of the boys, not tall and elegant like Sharyn.

She held out her hand for his torch, stalked around to the front of his car and peered under the hood. With an ease born of familiarity with machinery on the family property, she assessed the damage. "Your radiator's taken a beating as well as the bonnet. I doubt it will get you to Mt. Isa tonight. You do know you can't drive over eighty on these roads after dusk?"

"I doubt I was doing even that. The roo was going faster than me." Annoyance tinged his voice and he shoved his hands into his pockets. "Any chance I can catch a lift with you?"

The last thing Amy wanted was this prig invading her space. But leaving him by the side of the road waiting for another ride wasn't an option. She wouldn't leave her worst enemy in such a fix, and he was far from that. Even if he had smirked at her *wardrobe malfunction*. She shuddered as she imagined the phrase with Sharyn's intonation. "Hop in."

"Thank you." Stiff formality crackled in those two words.

Amy sniffed and thumbed the torch off. Let him be in a snit. Maybe he wouldn't want to talk as they drove, and that would suit her fine.

Dan reached into the boot for his medical bag. He needed travelling with the belligerent blonde like he needed a hole in the head. Petite and feisty, she clearly didn't want his company. Maybe Amy had been given the lowdown on him already. If his reason for leaving Gosford had been leaked to his new employer, he could hardly begin with a clean slate. The thought depressed him before he remembered her obvious embarrassment at the races.

A memory of white silk and tanned thighs rushed back as he thought of their unfortunate meeting, and he slammed the boot. Thank God she didn't realise how clearly her ute's lights had outlined her curves as she'd approached him. High heels had been replaced by a pair of unlaced work boots but headlights through her filmy skirt revealed far more than swirling wind. Better not share that titbit or she'd order him out of her car. Being stranded sucked, especially when he had several articles he needed to read before reporting for work tomorrow.

He climbed into the cabin and put his bag on the floor. Turning to her, he waited until she was seated and reached for her seatbelt. "I'm Dan. And you're Amy?"

"S'pose Mark told you. I'm surprised you noticed my face."

"Look, I'm sorry I laughed. I didn't intend to embarrass you." Another woman would have laughed off the incident, or played it up. Amy's response suggested she lacked confidence.

Not his problem.

In the soft glow of the dashboard light, her chin tipped higher and her knuckles tightened on the wheel. "Can we not mention that again?" She pulled out onto the highway.

"Consider the subject closed." But Amy was mistaken if she thought he'd forget her. He folded his arms across his chest and closed his eyes.

Thirty minutes later, lulled by the motion of the car and several poor nights' sleep, Dan woke with a start as Amy pulled into the first service station on the way into town. He sat up and rubbed the back of his neck.

"I've got to pick up a few groceries. Where do you want me to drop you off?" She opened her door and jumped out before turning and pinning him with her hazel gaze.

"Uh, I can catch a taxi from here."

Amy nodded, rummaged in the side pocket of the door and took out a business card, which she passed across the centre console. "If you're sure. That's for a towing company. Ask Derro to organise a tow for your car in the morning. Night."

Dan looked at the card before opening his door. "Thanks for the ride." He shoved the card in his shirt pocket, grabbed his bag and made for the taxi rank across the side street without looking back.

Under other circumstances, he might have asked Amy out to dinner. Just to say thanks. But she'd made it clear she didn't want to see him again. Which would make tomorrow very interesting.

Do you like your stories with a twist of suspense?
Read on for an introduction to *High Stakes*, romantic suspense set on the track to Mt Everest in Nepal.

Prologue

Sydney, Australia

John Chan faced his father across the antique rosewood desk. Eyes black and lustreless as coal pinned him to the parquet floor. Sleek, satin lapels contrasted with his snow-white tuxedo, and the benign smile he'd bestowed on guests gathered to celebrate his birthday in the marquee below was wiped from his face. Loss of face, especially for the eldest son of the head of family, was unacceptable. He bowed his head and waited for his father to pronounce sentence.

"You allowed her into your office because you let desire for this woman overrule your head. The woman accessed your computer. She escaped. We may be compromised."

"Father, I regret—"

"For a woman." Disgust leached through his words, pitching his voice higher than normal.

It didn't matter that John had increased profits since taking over operations in Sydney. Endangering the family and the business meant his life was forfeit. If his father so wished.

"Third Uncle wants your balls stuffed in your mouth. Second Uncle prefers a visit to the shark tank."

Of course. A bullet to his temple would be considered weakness.

Bile rose in John's throat. Hands gripped tightly together, he tried to swallow the lump of fear threatening to block his response. Now was not the time to show emotion. Now was the time for quick thinking, and for negotiation. What could he offer in exchange for his life?

"I have a contact in the Bureau. May I protect my family by accessing my resources?"

His father shifted on his seat. Red and gold brocade rustled, and shimmered in the low light preferred by his ageing eyes. He tapped one gnarled index finger on the wooden arm of the chair. When it stopped, John raised his eyes to meet his father's.

"Do this, and perhaps your uncles and I will let you live." His father dismissed him with a single flick of his hand. As though he was no more than a fly.

The woman he had sought to win as his mistress had brought him to this.

Anger seared his gut as John bowed and backed out of his father's office. Luxury and all the clothes wealth could afford had been offered but the woman had played him for a fool. Humiliation would be heaped on her tenfold. She would pay dearly.

He pulled his phone from his pocket and unlocked it with his thumbprint. Scrolling through his contacts, the tremor in his fingers filled him with shame. When the code name appeared, he stabbed the screen and waited. Hand in pocket, he peered through the window. Rivulets of rain blurred his view of the formal garden, and red Poinciana leaves bled into a green bush.

The connection rang four times, as it always did. "What do you want now? I told you, she went to the airport where our tail lost her."

His contact had never shown him respect. One day, when his usefulness was over, John would take pleasure in putting a bullet into Iceman's brain.

But not yet.

"You have one chance. Find her. Kill her."

Chapter One

Jake Harris crossed his scuffed trekking boots and touched his whisky glass to the UN commissioner's. Damn if the man didn't keep the best supply this side of Everest. He sipped, welcoming the burn of island peat on his tongue, down his throat, in his gut. Not one drop had touched his lips in two months. Not since he'd found his brother in the garage.

Hanging like a frozen side of beef.

Dead.

The memory slammed through him with the force of an avalanche, and the whisky soured in the black pit of his soul.

Peter. Baby brother. Coke-head.

Dead.

He set the crystal tumbler on the mahogany desk with a thunk. Lamplight lit the lower half of his body and he leaned back, praying his face was in deep shadow. If—when—he got his hands on those responsible for Pete's death, he'd bring them down. By any means. "What do you need from me, Mr Nicholls?"

Grey jacket sleeves rode up and revealed pristine white cuffs. The commissioner folded soft hands on the desk, and his socially-polite, upwardly-mobile smile, the smile of the career diplomat, was packed away. "I understand you're a man of few words. I suppose that's why you chose field work over the diplomatic corps."

The commissioner's plummy tones grated. Jake preferred

lilting Nepalese voices to Oxford city-slickness. "I'm leaving Kathmandu in the morning."

"Impatient, Mr Harris?"

"I have new field agents to train." In truth, his second-in-charge in the south-east Asia division of the Bureau was responsible for inductions, but Jake needed space. Room to breathe, open air, and pushing himself to the limit so he could snatch a few hours of dreamless sleep. So far the plan had failed more than it had succeeded.

"Fine, let's cut to the chase. Doctor Westcott is heading up the trail towards Everest Base Camp. Ostensibly on holiday." Nicholls drew a folder towards him.

"And?"

"It's the second part of her trip we hold concerns about."

"Congratulations on solving all the major world problems." He didn't bother trying to subdue his sarcastic side. Sarcasm was good. Sarcasm masked his I'm-going-through-hell face and made taking his next breath, and the next, and the next, possible.

Bitter sarcasm was all he had left.

Because he'd failed. Failed to protect one of the few people he cared about.

Nicholls' hooded eyes fixed on Jake and the sharp plane of his nose lowered as if he were a bird dropping from the sky on hapless prey. Jake glared right back at the commissioner and to hell with protocol. He didn't give a damn if he pissed the man off. He didn't give a damn about anything.

Nicholls fiddled with the knot of his tie. "Doctor Westcott has applied for a research permit to visit the Dolpa region." Jake flicked through memories of his only trip to the central province. "It's remote, difficult to access, and entry permits are expensive and restricted. Not many trekkers go there. What's the concern?"

"Her specialty. Biological chemistry."

"So? I don't see the connection."

Nicholls leaned back and a smug smile tugged at the corners

of his mouth. "Need to know basis, Harris."

Jake thought about telling Nicholls to take his intrigue and shove it where the sun didn't shine. The words teetered on the springboard of his tongue, raw, harsh, bitter. He couldn't give a flying fuck. Not when he had a mountain of paperwork, and a group of raw recruits to whip into shape. "I'm head of drug enforcement operations for the region. Who the hell do you think needs to know if not me?"

Nicholls pursed his lips and tapped his fingers on the closed folder. "This case requires top security clearance."

"Which I have. So—she's a biological chemist. What's the connection?"

"Her work involves research and synthesising compounds."

"Making what? Who for, and why here?"

"That's the problem; we don't know."

"Is Doctor Westcott flying in or trekking?"

Nicholls' internal struggle—to stand firm or answer—drew twin lines of battle between his eyebrows. "What difference does it make?"

A flicker of pleasure licked through Jake. Poncy desk jockey didn't know everything. "Have you ever trekked, Mr Nicholls?"

"Not really my cup of tea." Nicholls' clipped tone dismissed the absurd notion. He picked up a pen and patterned the print label on the folder in a series of jabs. The pen stopped, point down amid a mess of blue dots.

"Why is her mode of travel important?" The question was dragged from him like a dentist pulling a bad tooth.

Jake reached for his glass and took a leisurely mouthful. Nicholls' ignorance of transport within Nepal betrayed his inexperience, but it gave Jake the edge to prise out more details about the woman.

"How she travels determines how much and what can be carried. Unless I know more about what I'm meant to be looking for, I can't help you." He tossed back the last mouthful of whisky.

"That's a smooth drop. Don't mind if I have another." Warmth spread through his belly and he poured two fingers' into his glass and sat back.

An antique clock chimed the quarter hour and the echoes hung heavily as Nicholls appeared to deliberate. Finally, he spoke. "Drugs."

The single word blazed like a neon light in the night. Jake's breath caught on the sharp rock of grief lodged in his throat, his stomach clenched. His hands fisted on his knees, and a bongo-beat accelerated in his brain: *Revenge—Peter—revenge—Peter—revenge.*

"You were instrumental in breaking up an international supply line out of Afghanistan last month. I believe the leader, Al-Kohari was killed?"

"Yes." The word shot out like the bullet that put the drug lord beyond reach of justice. The legal kind, at least. Jake's only regret was Al-Kohari had been the key to finding and proving the Australian connection. Without him . . .

Nicholls leaned back. "Nepal isn't exactly drug territory but if Doctor Westcott is involved, we need to know."

"If she's involved, I'll bring her in."

Nicholls capped the pen. "The doctor dined with John Chan in Sydney a few days before she arrived in Kathmandu. Chan is the eldest son of a family with Asian drug links. He met the doctor at an upmarket restaurant on Sydney's Circular Quay."

Jake's heart stuttered then began a mad thumping. The Chan cartel was likely Peter's supplier. He could still see his younger brother's face, purple and obscene above the noose. Jake forced his lungs to breathe. His hand clenched the glass and he downed the whisky in a single mouthful.

"This was taken by an undercover agent tailing Chan." Nicholls opened the folder and handed over an enlarged photo.

Beneath heavy, long, black curls, the woman's delicate expression appeared intent on her dinner companion. She was beautiful. His dispassionate gaze began cataloguing details; from the tilt of her head to the thigh-high slit in her black dress, sex appeal oozed from the woman.

"You said she was dining with Chan. Do you think it was business or pleasure?" Jake tipped the photo towards the desk lamp. "Have you got a magnifier?"

Nicholls took an old-fashioned magnifying glass from his drawer and handed it across the desk. "By the look of her I'd say pleasure, but this was the only time the operative saw them alone together."

Jake examined the photograph closely, paying attention to a mark on the woman's thigh, visible in the thigh-split of the slim-fitting black dress.

A tattoo. Maybe a snake or a gecko. He studied her features, memorising them. Any link to the Chans ensured he would take on this assignment. "So how does her trip to Dolpa fit in with this Sydney drug cartel?"

"We suspect a connection. Her visa states the trip is for research. Loopholes in the laws of both our countries allow the legal importation of certain *natural* drugs, which are then recombined. Some of the ingredients in recombined form are responsible for the recent spate of deaths in your capital cities. And mine."

Jake set the photo and magnifier on the desk. "The Chans are at the centre of it?"

"In Sydney, almost certainly."

"Paul Rimmer and I worked undercover in Sydney before I was promoted to head up the Asian bureau. At last contact, he hinted he was onto someone involved in the local trade."

And now Nicholls was handing him a connection to that underworld family. If it was the last thing he did he would find this woman who had allied herself with the Chinese drug cartel and he would extract the truth. And if she was involved in manufacturing and research . . . Jake's hand fisted on his knee.

"Too many young lives are being cut short." Nicholls' comment lacked real emotion. But bureaucratic say-the-right-thing blah hit Jake hard.

Peter would never grow up, grow old, grow anything. He had ceased to exist except in Jake's memory, and as a black and white statistic on a government department's page.

Grief sank in Paul's gut like a boulder, free-falling down—down—down—into a bottomless chasm.

But he couldn't afford the luxury of time to grieve. Time in which the drug family would set up a new supplier, find new supply lines, shatter more families. He pulled himself together, locked his grief down tighter than an airport on terrorist alert. Peter's death would not go unavenged.

"So this doctor is working for the cartel?"

"That, Harris, is what we want you to find out. Observation only for the time being, but we want to know what the Dolpa connection is. If you confirm a link to the Chans, bring her in." Nicholls closed the folder and shoved it across the desk. "We want eyes on her as soon as possible, before she makes contact with anyone. How quickly can you reach Everest Base Camp?"

"I'll fly in by helicopter tomorrow and backtrack until I find her. Before she reaches Everest, I'll catch her."

And if the doctor was working for the drug family, he would make her pay.

You can find the book here: http://amzn.to/2Ek44Y4

I hope you enjoyed your introduction to Lark Creek! If you would like to share the love and leave a review, I would be grateful. And if you would like to know when a new book is releasing:

You can find me at the following:

a. Facebook https://www.facebook.com/susanne.bellamy.7
b. Twitter   https://twitter.com/SusanneBellamy
c. Website http://www.susannebellamy.com/
d. Pinterest http://www.pinterest.com/susannebellamy/
e. Goodreads
   https://www.goodreads.com/author/list/6869630.Susanne
   Bellamy

Or on my website: http://www.susannebellamy.com

www.ingramcontent.com/pod-product-compliance
Lightning Source LLC
Chambersburg PA
CBHW030645110726
47901CB00002B/579